Norman Does It Again!!!! Another Five Star!

Once again, Danielle Norman has left me itching for more. Getting Even is a phenomenal start to the Iron Ladies series. It is fun, fast paced and has tough as nails ladies, that you can't help but love!

— ☆☆☆☆☆ REVIEWER

Another Awesome Read

Another great book by Danielle Norman. I first met her ladies in the Iron Badges series. The characters crossover from all the Iron series. Her ladies are fun and sassy.

— ☆☆☆☆☆ REVIEWER

ADELINE, GETTING EVEN

Iron Ladies

DANIELLE NORMAN

COPYRIGHT

Reviews are Important

HEY, don't forget to leave a review when you're done reading. Here are perks exclusive to Danielle fans only, bwahaha

AT 250 REVIEWS- you get a lifetime subscription of the sugar free, knock-off version of Oreos called Whoreos. Did you read that wrong? It is Who reos, get your mind out of the gutter.

AT 500 REVIEWS- Tiny leprechauns dressed up as Thunder Down Under give live performances FREE for all of my fans.

AT 1000 REVIEWS- A UNICORN jumps out of every book and lulls you to sleep with a lullaby before shanking anyone that karma forgot with its horn.

I'd like to dedicate this to all the firsts.
The first husbands and first wives that thought the grass was greener
in someone else's fucking yard.
As a second wife, I thank you for being a ho.
The first glass of vodka after a shitty day.
And...
The first roll of your eyes after hearing someone say something
absolutely stupid and then giving yourself a high-five for not throat
punching them.

So, let me be the first to raise my glass to you and say, "Thank you."

In the quest for happily ever after; it isn't about being someone's first love. It's about being their last love.

— UNKNOWN

PROLOGUE

welve years ago . . .

ADELINE TOSSED her hair over her shoulder, took a deep breath, and told herself she could do this.

She had to.

It was this or drugs, and she knew all too well that drugs weren't an option.

"It seemed like I was always trying to live up to my parents' expectations. I had to be perfect, you know? Perfect daughter, perfect grades, perfect everything. Sometimes the pressure just got to be too much and I needed an escape. In my head, I knew it was wrong, but at the same time there was the little voice coaxing me, telling me hey, *who's it gonna hurt? What they didn't know wouldn't hurt them*. It helped at first to take the edge off, but then I realized I was not only hurting myself, but also everyone around me."

"Thank you, Adeline, for sharing your story with us. Let's end here today, everyone. Thank you for making the commitment to yourselves to be here. I know that some days it seems easier to throw in the towel, but every day you are proving how strong you really are."

The members of the Heal Your Soul therapy group dispersed. It was the fifty-second day of Adeline's three-month-long rehabilitation program, and she and the other participants had been brought together for group. This week, the theme had been: "Shared experiences lighten the burdens."

True to the counselor's words, Adeline Morgan did feel like a boulder had been lifted off her chest. She had to admit, rehab hadn't been such a bad idea after all.

She was willing to do anything to avoid the prescribed SSRIs, they made her feel like a zombie, and besides, Adeline knew herself, knew that she and meds did not get along. The group had been a great help, and sharing her pains and experiences with the others had made her feel better, as if she wasn't alone. Everyone had a story to tell, they were different, but just as painful. Adeline's had been filled with disappointments from loved ones.

There was only one drawback after days like today, when it was her turn to share a part of her story—her nightmares. Adeline walked the sage-colored hallways, not bothering to check out the generic inspirational posters or hotel-esque artwork, and made it back to her private room without ever having to acknowledge anyone else.

The room housed one bed and one small, three-drawer dresser, but she didn't care. Not having a roommate had been one of the conditions of her agreeing to the program. She refused to be saddled with someone who was legitimately nuts and kept her up all night. Plus, it wasn't as if her parents couldn't afford it or that she was permitted to do anything or have any possessions with her. Plus, she didn't spend all that much time in it anyway.

The schedule at the center kept the patients occupied almost every minute of the day, so Adeline only had ten minutes to get ready before lights were out. Pulling the covers down, Adeline crawled into the bed. Her heart was already racing a million miles a minute because she knew that as soon as she closed her eyes, the memories would creep in. She didn't want to fall asleep, which was the heart of the problem. Why she turned to drugs in the first place.

Like every night since she got there, she tried fighting the drowsiness by rehashing where she'd went wrong, what could she have done differently? All the missteps she had taken. It seemed like yesterday that Adeline was bringing home a report card for her mother to look at.

"We're so proud of you Adeline." Mrs. Morgan snapped a photo of Adeline's report card to post on Facebook. Adeline's mother had always done this, because she saw her daughter's grades as a direct reflection on herself.

Then she'd hand her card over to her dad, who would coach her on ways to be even better. "Remember you need to have a strong academic and social life to get into Harvard like your old man." Mr. Morgan took a seat and lifted his glass of scotch in emphasis.

"I know, Dad. I have cheerleading again as well as chorus this year. Plus, I have student government, and I have signed up for the debate team."

Adeline wanted to be perfect, the most popular, the best daughter, and she had almost achieved it. She thought she had for a short while, like when the announcer had called her name as prom queen and her long-time high school boyfriend as prom king. Adeline stood on stage and waved to her class-mates, and her heart was warmed by the genuine happiness that she saw in her best friend Sasha's eyes when Sasha looked up at the stage.

Perfection had been the keyword for Adeline growing up.

Her parents preached it daily, and she had lived by that principle until . . . well . . . she revolted.

And Adeline discovered that some parents have a breaking point . . .

Prom night was the game changer. Mark was nowhere to be found, so Adeline decided to have Sasha take her home, but Sasha was nowhere to be found either. Looking back, Adeline knew it was all a little too cliché because she found them . . . *together* in the backseat of Sasha's car.

It was the catalyst that sent Adeline spiraling. In typical teenager fashion, she told everyone that Mark had been cheating on her with Sasha, and while Mark's involvement was barely noted, Sasha became a social pariah.

Adeline had laughed, feeling vindication. After all, what Sasha had done was beyond reprehensible. Her best friend had broken her trust and deserved whatever came her way.

Then, about a month before graduation, Sasha Dexter committed suicide.

And it wasn't so damn funny anymore.

All the sleepovers.

All the birthday parties.

Years of exchanging friendship bracelets.

The promise of BFF forever.

All ruined, all lost, over a few bad decisions.

Her parents used words like, *bounce back*, *get over it*, and *move on*. They expected her to still uphold the Morgan family values. But once again, she'd disappointed them.

Adeline reached for the bottle of water on her nightstand and drank. What she really wanted was the burn from whiskey. The fuzzy pull of whatever painkiller she could get her hands on.

Adeline closed her eyes and inhaled, sleep finally overtaking her.

And a cold chill crawled up her as Adeline blamed Mark

and all men like him. If he hadn't tried to play friends against each other. If he hadn't been such a no-good, two-timing asshole, if he hadn't been such a...guy. Then maybe Sasha would still be here and maybe Adeline would still have parents that acknowledged her as their only child. Maybe, just maybe, things would have turned out for the better.

∾

AT THE THREE-MONTH MARK, Adeline left rehab a changed woman, albeit not much older in age but older in wisdom. Those three months had matured Adeline more than the last five years had since graduating high school.

But now she felt like she had a purpose. After listening to all the stories from women who'd been broken by the men they'd trusted she was determined to make a difference. She didn't get into Harvard, but she did enroll in college. Her course focus would be criminal justice.

Unfortunately, Adeline found herself alone on a giant campus. She was older and wiser than most of the other freshmen on campus. She watched as they explored the freedom of being away from home for the first time, drinking and experimenting with things she knew were a slippery slope. Every night she went home to the large house her parents had gifted to her, their way of alleviating the guilt of not allowing her back into their home and their lives. They'd had enough of her drama and truthfully, she couldn't blame them. But Adeline was determined to prove to them that she wasn't the fuck up they'd written her off as, and maybe, just maybe, someday they'd pick up her phone call.

But college was where Adeline's life seemed to fall into place. It was where she met her new best friends: Melanie Oakes, who had fought to stand out in her male-dominated house; Sunday Prescott, who lacked male attention until one day she caught the attention of the campus playboy only to discover it was all a joke; and Olivia Vinning, who was raised in a violent home.

Three women studying for criminal-justice degrees, and one night over drinks Adeline shared her dream. Together they'd start a whispered network for women. Their rules were simple: one must receive the orchid-colored business card from a previous client to even know that they exist, because they weren't your normal private investigators. They were the Iron Ladies.

Chapter One

ADELINE

$\mathcal{T}$he screeching sound of the tires as the V8 American muscle car pulled into a parking space in one fell swoop was one of Adeline Morgan's favorite sounds in the world. The only thing better than that was shopping.

She sat in her seat a few minutes and let the song, which was playing far too loudly, finish before she cut the engine. The abrupt absence of the rumble and music in the afternoon air hit Adeline like a shiver of anxiety. There was a comfort in all things car and speed, but she was late, so she forced herself not to crank the engine again.

Adeline pushed the solid steel door open and slid from her seat before straightening her black bodycon dress, which clung to her curvy figure. Then she slipped her four-inch black leather heels back on—one did not drive a muscle car with heels on—and grabbed the bags from the passenger seat.

The Iron Ladies office took up the majority of the fourth floor of one of the many tall buildings in downtown Orlando, and it was more of a home to her than her actual house was. The main office, like other rooms in the company, stood immaculate, with white walls and floor-to-ceiling windows that revealed a large view of the city.

Adeline walked past the desks that sat in an open floor plan and into the boardroom. A large oil painting of giant handcuffs hung on the opposite wall, and in the center of the room was a large mahogany table. Around said table were some unhappy faces. Well, all except Melanie, she was pacing the room.

"Where the fuck have you been?" Melanie stopped pacing long enough to glare at Adeline. "Really? The client's been waiting nearly an hour."

Adeline shrugged and had a shit-eating grin on her face as she fell into her seat next to Sunday before setting her bags onto the table in front of her. "Sorry, my lunch break lasted longer than usual."

"Told you so," Sunday said, a little too happy.

Adeline winked at Sunday. "No one knows me better than you do."

"Depends what truck stop we go to, I'm sure there's a few bathrooms that have poetry written in your honor and we could learn a thing or two." Olivia reached into her pocket, pulled out some money, and handed it over to Sunday, obviously having lost a bet. Sunday grinned triumphantly, tossed Adeline half the take, and turned back to her laptop.

Adeline flipped Olivia off and laughed, knowing full well that Olivia's harsh barb was only a joke.

"Well, now that we're finally all here, can we interview the client already?" Melanie asked, glaring between the two of them.

"Fine by me," Sunday said, clearly not really paying attention, she was too absorbed in her computer.

"Who's the client anyway?" Adeline asked.

"Some lady." Sunday never lifted her eyes from her laptop screen.

Adeline rolled her eyes. "You think? I was assuming that we were still Iron Ladies and not men. But, then again, maybe you all voted to change that while I was out."

Olivia sighed. "How about I bring her in for the interview, and thereafter you two can argue about whatever gender you think the client is?"

"Whoa, someone's in a bad mood today." Adeline let out a low whistle.

"Adeline, you're late . . . again. You come in here with this I-don't-care attitude. But, damn it, I know you well enough to know that, if I look in those bags, there is probably something for me in there that I'm going to love." Olivia slapped her hands onto the table as Adeline leaned forward, reached into the aforementioned bags, and pulled out the most awesome black leather vest.

"I'll get her." Melanie headed toward the boardroom doors. "And for goodness' sake, Olivia. Put that thing away."

"Yeah, Olivia, put that thing away." Adeline smiled as Olivia gathered her oil rag and kit to start reassembling her baby Glock.

One of their founding and non-negotiable rules was that all four members had to be present for the first meet with all potential clients. The rule had been Melanie's idea, and according to her, it presented a professional and united front to the client. Melanie had also stressed the importance of making a good first impression on the client, which was another important reason for all members to be present for first contact. Finally, all four members had to state their opinion and cast their vote on whether they should take the case. Majority always won. The rules may sound stupid, but it was these cornerstones that had made the Iron Ladies an underground success. Oh, to most, they were just everyday businesswomen, but to the women who were passed the orchid-colored card, they were more than that.

When Melanie returned with their client, Adeline let out a muted groan. It was Loren fucking Delaney. She was everything that Adeline knew her to be—cultured, elegant, collected, classy, and the fucking mayor of Orlando's wife.

"We apologize for the delay, Mrs. Delaney." Melanie ushered Loren to a seat at the head of the table. Melanie, Sunday, and Olivia cast glances at Adeline. "I don't suppose you've met our fourth member Adeline yet?"

"Hello, Adeline, it's nice to meet you. Thank you all for agreeing to meet me." Loren gave a wave to Adeline, and Adeline returned it with a slight smile.

"Do you have something for us?" Adeline asked.

"Oh, yes, I do." Loren reached into her purse and pulled out the secret orchid colored business card, it was the only proof that the Iron Ladies existed. They didn't advertise, they weren't listed in a phonebook, nor did they have a website. They operated simply by referrals. Melanie took the card.""So, Mrs. Delaney—"

"Please, call me Loren."

"Okay," Melanie continued. "Loren, since you contacted us, I take it you were given our card by one of your friends."

"Yes, by—"

Melanie held up one hand to stop Loren from continuing. "Please, we keep everyone's privacy."

Loren nodded her understanding.

"Then you also understand that this meeting is an interview and not a guarantee that we will take your case?"

Loren folded her hands in her lap, but Adeline paid close attention to the slight shake of her shoulders.

"You are aware that we are not your normal private investigator service? As such, our fees reflect our exceptional services."

Again, Loren nodded. "I really do hope that you take my case, though."

Sunday looked away from her computer and met Loren's eyes. "As you're aware, one of our services includes helping women whose husbands are . . . assholes?" Loren suppressed a laugh. "Since you're here, I'm assuming that the mayor has been very, ummm, assholey?"

"To say the least," Loren concurred.

"We need you to tell us why you are here." Melanie shot Adeline a glare for not waiting her turn.

"Please excuse my colleague," Melanie snapped. "We aren't trying to rush you."

"Well. . . actually, I kinda am," Adeline quipped.

"Adeline." Melanie gritted her teeth.

"He's the fucking mayor, that spells trouble." A big part of the Iron Ladies' success was dependent on staying below the radar, and there was nothing above the radar more than a fucking politician.

Olivia interrupted, "I think most of the talking needs to come from Loren."

"Agreed." Melanie nodded.

Loren looked down at her hands as if she was contemplating each word. "I met Greg when I was an intern at his law office. I like to think I was actually on my way to being a talented lawyer, but when Greg made me an offer to work alongside him in his organization, I took it without hesitation." Loren paused to study the faces of her audience.

"Go on, Loren," Adeline encouraged her.

"So, I worked for him as an intern. At first, I was intimidated by him since he had such a temper. You know, one moment calm and the next, there were papers and objects flying across the room. He got stirred up by the littlest things. He hid it well, and only those closest to him ever saw it. Everyone else thought he was perfect. I knew he had goals to run for office, so I overlooked a lot because I knew it would be great for my career." Loren laughed, but it was a watery sound that had Olivia passing over the box of tissues they kept in the room for just that reason.

"Thank you." Loren wiped her tears and forced a tight smile. "I'm fine. Anyway . . ." She pulled in a calming breath. "We started dating a few months after I took the job, and a year later, we were married. I genuinely thought that he had loved me, but all he really loved was what I did for his image. It took me five years to figure out that the only reason he married me was because he needed a wife who fit the ideal image for his political aspirations." Loren played with the tissue in her hands, and slowly shredded it without realizing her actions. "Our marriage, it isn't real, nothing about it is real. We never talk, well, not unless we are in public, then he seems interested in me. He's a good actor . . ." Loren let out a chuckle. "Even I was fooled. Occasionally, we had sex . . . plain old vanilla, emotionless sex. But that isn't even once a month. We all know that if he isn't getting it at home, he's getting it somewhere. Every time I try to ask him about it or even ask him if he's coming home, he goes off on me. We are probably up to World War eighteen thousand in our house. Everything turns into a war."

Adeline leaned forward and gave Loren's arm a reassuring squeeze.

"The thing is, I'm tired of the pretense, of the coldness. I want a real marriage, not just something that appears perfect from the outside. I want to be happy. I want my daughter to be happy. I've endured all this time because of my little girl, and I've realized that she shouldn't be in a loveless family. I want to teach her that she deserves to be loved."

"Have you called an attorney? Why not just file for a divorce?"

Loren grabbed another tissue and played with it like a worry stone. "No, I haven't, because as soon as he catches wind of this, I won't be able to fight him. If there is anything in this world Greg cherishes, it's his reputation, and guys like Greg don't allow their wives to leave them. It's as much about control as it is anything else."

This was always Adeline's least favorite part of the interview process, not because she hated meeting new clients, but because this was when it felt like pulling teeth just to get a straight answer. Nothing was short and to the point.

"Do you think that Greg would try and hurt you if he found out?"

"Not physically hurt me, but I need you to know that Greg is up for reelection and he has aspirations for governor someday. He views appearances as a vital part of his image. His career comes before anybody else. He can be ruthless, and when this all blows over, he isn't going to spare me. If I don't have enough evidence against him, then he will use his clout to make the courts view me as a bad mother. He doesn't want custody of Noelle, our daughter, but he'll do it just to hurt me and try to control me. Noelle is scared of him, she hides from him because he screams all the time. I desperately need your help."

Something in Adeline's gut was telling her that this case was a hard no, it was spelling trouble. "What do you think we might be able to find about Greg, what kind of evidence?"

"My grandparents owned a lot of property around central Florida and they left me a parcel of about five-thousand acres as part of my trust. It has been valued at about five million dollars and is prime real estate. Just before Greg and I got married, I had an attorney set it up for a trust for our first child. Once Noelle was born, I had her name put on the property. I asked Greg about it a few months ago, because I didn't get a tax bill this year. It always comes in my name as the custodian for Noelle. He said he'd look into it, but when I asked about it again he got mad at me. So, I went to the property appraiser's page and looked up the information, but the info was hidden."

"Hidden?"

"Yeah, hidden. You can file to have your property address hidden on all tax records and your driver's license if you're law enforcement or in a government position. It keeps people from looking you up and then showing up at your house. Our home address is hidden, but I couldn't have the land done since it was under my maiden name and Noelle's name."

"So, what are you suggesting?"

"I'm not entirely sure. I just know that something isn't right about the situation, and no one at the property appraiser's office will release any information to me."

"But, you're the owner of the property, right? Why wouldn't they talk to you about it?"

"I don't know. All I know is that when I couldn't find anything online, I called them, and the man who answered told me that he couldn't give me any information because of the Privacy Act. I tried to explain to him that he didn't need to protect my own privacy from me, but he apologized again and hung up."

"And you think that Greg has done something behind your back?" Adeline asked.

"Yes. In fact, I'm almost positive, because I overheard a conversation he had with someone. He was on the phone one night and I heard him talking about the land. That was the night before I called you. He's the mayor, if he catches on to any of this he will discredit me, so before I do anything, I need proof that he's having an affair for the prenuptial. I need proof of his temper to keep him from taking my daughter, and I need to find out what he did with my inheritance. He is underhanded. I don't want him to be able to turn people against me and blame it on me just being a bitter woman. I want undeniable proof that he's a cheating, underhanded asshole."

Olivia, Sunday, Adeline, and Melanie were silent for a second, waiting to see if Loren had any other bombs to drop. When the woman just continued to fidget, Melanie smiled and stood.

"Thank you, Loren, you've given us a lot to consider. We need to discuss what you've told us and do a little research on our own before we can give you our answer. We, of course, will try to get back to you as soon as possible and will keep you posted about our next meeting with you." Melanie shook Loren's hand across the table. Adeline, Sunday, and Olivia followed suit, each extending a hand one at a time to Loren.

"It was nice having this opportunity with all of you. I really hope you consider this . . . if not for me, for my daughter."

Melanie held the boardroom doors open and escorted Loren out. When the doors shut, Adeline, Sunday, and Olivia sighed in unison.

"Holy fucking shit. Loren Delaney, who would have thought?" Adeline shook her head, not believing what she had just witnessed. "On television and in the newspapers, they come across as being a happy couple. Just goes to show you that there's no such thing as a perfect marriage. What's this world coming to when women that look like fucking June Cleaver can't keep a man? I can see the tagline now, don't take it so hard Beaver."

Olivia turned to stare at Adeline, her mouth agape. "I have no fucking clue where you come up with this shit."

Adeline shrugged her shoulders. "It's a gift, what can I say?"

Melanie shook her head. "Well, let's get back to business, you know the drill." She arched one eyebrow and locked eyes with Adeline. "What do you think? It seems like you're against us helping her, Adeline." Melanie made a few notes in her notebook.

"Trouble. Politicians are all trouble. He's going to have every city office coming down on us. We are going to lose our business license and the fire marshal is suddenly going to find fifty things to fine us over before shutting us down."

"I think she needs our help and we can give it," Olivia explained.

"Don't they all?" Adeline asked.

Sunday peered over her laptop. "I liked her."

Adeline gave her a deadpan look. "I'd like to meet a client you *didn't* like. You do know we can't save them all, right?"

"Way to have a positive outlook there, Adeline." Olivia threw her hands up in the air. "Debbie downer...she delivers."

"Say what you want, Olivia, but it's shit like Greg Delaney that use their connections to rule with an iron fist. He will make an example out of us and his wife."

"Okay, Adeline, we've heard your side." Melanie turned her attention to Sunday. "What are your thoughts?"

Sunday shrugged. "I've got a feeling, I'll have the votes on my side."

Adeline scoffed. "Livi, what do you think?"

"Politician's wife. Payment shouldn't be a problem."

Melanie chewed on her lower lip. "Maybe. . .then again he could be keeping her on a tight leash."

"Love is the issue with her, not money," Sunday said, defending her stance.

Adeline shook her head. "We don't know that. Hell, for all we know Loren could be a great liar and actress."

"Adeline, let Loren worry about how Loren pays, okay? We've got shit to do, as long as she can cover the deposit. Besides, there's always Coco's."

"Thank god for Coco," they all said in unison. Coco was

the owner of Queen's Gold, a notorious pawn shop in downtown Orlando.

"Coco may not be all that willing to help Loren though, you know how she feels about cops. I don't think she holds much more respect for our Mayor Greg Delaney either."

"Well, depending on the vote, let's see what Loren comes up with first," Sunday explained.

"Sounds to me that Sunday is in favor of helping Loren. Is that right?" Melanie turned to Sunday and Sunday nodded.

"Who else is in favor of Loren?" Melanie held up her hand along with Olivia.

"Not me." Adeline was the only one not agreeing. Everyone turned to stare at Adeline, amazed since she usually was the first one to want to defend all women.

"You've got a knack for being the odd one, don't you?" Melanie shook her head, once again shocked by Adeline.

"What? I don't like politicians. They're grabby. They're self-righteous, and chances are I'll have to get up close and personal with this one." Adeline shivered at the thought.

"I say we help her. She needs us, and it is our job to help those who need us. Will it be risky? Yes, but that will only help us in the long run. We will prove hands down that no one in Central Florida is above us or above being busted by us. Think about it, the rumor mill that will be sparked when someone actually catches Greg Delaney red-handed..."

"How about you, Olivia?"

"She's got a kid. If it was just her, then I'd weigh whether it was worth going against someone who had that much power and money, but there's a kid involved. We do it."

Adeline flicked her nails nonchalantly, as though it was no big deal that the others weren't agreeing with her. "What about you, Mel? What are your thoughts?"

"I think that while we are getting evidence to help protect Loren, we gather a little extra to protect ourselves. You know? Call it an insurance policy. He comes after us, then no matter what happens between him and Loren, we have material to ruin him."

Sunday clapped her hands together. "Let's catch the lyin' lion."

"Outfox the fox," Olivia added.

"A lion wouldn't cheat, but a Tiger Wood."

"Ohhh, that was baddddd." They all groaned and turned to Adeline.

"What?" Adeline asked, feigning surprise. "Why are you looking at me?"

The other three let out sighs. Whether they admitted it or not, they all kind of loved Adeline just the way she was.

"Since the majority has spoken, you know the rules and will have to learn to cope with your feelings. It is all hands on deck. We're going to have to do more digging than usual. I have a feeling that Mayor Delaney is especially skilled at hiding his tracks." Everyone agreed with Melanie's announcement.

"Sunday?" Melanie went down her list of notes she'd made.

"Yes, homie?"

"You're gonna arrange a meeting with Loren at the country club, you're also gonna let her know about our retainer fee."

"At least make it our elevated fee," Adeline chimed in.

"Fifteen thousand?" Sunday asked.

Adeline nodded and so did Melanie and Olivia.

"Consider it done." Sunday gave a mock salute.

"Tires and bullets aren't cheap these days, you know? And besides we're not messing around on this one," Adeline defended her reasoning.

"Everyone got their jobs?" Melanie looked at Olivia and Adeline.

"I'll head over toward the mayor's office and start scouting the area. I'll upload photos as soon as I discover anything of use."

"I'll start trying to find out where he hangs out and if he's into brunettes?" Adeline patted her perfectly coifed hair as she headed out to her car.

More than anything Adeline would like to throw on a helmet and straddle a motorcycle, but that was unladylike, and part of their formula for success was to maintain an elevated lady-like appearance in public. Her only public rebellion was her cars. Adeline blamed it on *tools of the trade*. As the lead tactical driver and instructor for evasive driving maneuvers, Adeline claimed to need powerful cars, and nothing screamed power like good old American heavy duty V8 muscle cars. Plus, often times they provided the added bonus of opening conversations with their targets.

Adeline pulled into a parking lot across from City Hall and parked. She slid on her Zoomies, one of the greatest inventions for a private eye or peeping Tom, take your pick, since the hands-free binoculars looked like nothing more than ordinary glasses. Adeline reclined a bit in her seat, turned on her tunes, and watched the front doors and parking lot of the mayor's office. She needed to establish a routine for the mayor.

Chapter Two

RILEY

"*R*eally, it's seven o'clock in the fucking morning. Parents need to teach their kids some fucking manners." Riley's mood had been shot ever since his sister had called him last night and asked him to come over this morning but refused to tell him why. All she said was, "*Don't say anything to Greg.*"

He stayed up half the night worried that his baby sister had cancer, or that something was wrong with his niece. They were the only family he had left. "Now I'm even more on-edge, thanks to some asshat punk who doesn't realize he can fucking listen to music below eighty-five decibels."

"I'm sorry, did you say something?"

Riley looked up at the sultry voice and saw the real-life version of a wet dream. She was gorgeous and had curves he could grab on to. He was so busy picturing exactly how he would grab her that he hadn't even realized that the ear-rattling music had ended. He was more shocked that the gorgeous woman was staring at him, then he realized she was waiting for an answer.

"Oh no, sorry. I was just talking to myself."

"Yeah I heard . . . asshat punk." The sultry-voiced vixen smiled at him, then stepped back so Riley could get a good view of the V8 muscle car that had rolled in with music blaring, the one he'd assumed belonged to an asshat punk. "Don't blame it on my parents, they gave up on me years ago." The woman winked at him and then removed the gas pump from her car and put it back onto the holder before strutting off.

Yes, she fucking strutted.

Riley rolled his eyes. "Way to go. Way to fucking go." Returning his gas pump to the holder, he headed inside to grab his coffee and groaned when he saw her smirking at him.

"Don't tell me you've come to give me a hard time for adulterating this fine cup of joe." She held up a cup that was indeed destroyed in Riley's book; it had shit in it. Riley liked his coffee black. If he wanted a dessert, then he'd fucking buy a dessert, but coffee was a drink, it was meant to wake you up, and that shit she held in front of him definitely wouldn't.

"You think that the world revolves around you, don't you? You blare your music at a ridiculous level, not even considering that other people might be trying to have a conversation."

"What? In their car? You mean, talking on their phone while driving? I consider what I'm doing a public safety measure, they can put the phone down."

"Then you stand around just waiting to harass the next person that walks into a store and shove your coffee in their face."

"No, not the next person, just you. I was hoping that you would come in. You really are cute when you get angry, and I wanted to see if I could do it again. Remember? I'm all about public safety. Women should know what they're getting into with you."

"Let me guess, you're single. Oh, wait, I've got it . . . divorced. You ran him off, didn't you?"

The sexy woman flexed her fingers so he couldn't help but notice her blood-red nails. "No, I buried him after I took him to the cleaners. Looking for a wife?" She turned and strode off, only stopping long enough to throw some money onto the counter. He watched her as she strode across the parking lot, slid into her car, and—

"Excuse me, you gonna make your coffee or not?"

Riley looked over at the teenager, who looked way too young to be drinking coffee, and scoffed before he fixed his cup and got in line to pay.

Damn it, why did she have to be so sexy? He had a horrid track record when it came to sexy women, they usually ended being raving bitches or psycho-freaks. His luck, she'd probably end up being a psychotic-freaking-bitch.

HE SAT in his truck in front of his sister's large two-story Georgian home and made a few phone calls to ensure that his guys had everything under control, since odds were, he wouldn't be out to the property today.

Once he was sure the job wasn't going to go to hell, he headed around the house to the kitchen door. Riley raised his hand to knock but froze at the sound of a scream. Peering into the window, he saw his four-year-old niece crying on the kitchen floor. Riley lightly tapped on the window to get her attention and waved for her to come let him in. When she unlocked the door, he scooped her up, wrapped a firm hand around her head, and held her against his chest.

"Shhh, it's going to be okay." He didn't have to ask what was wrong, he could hear for himself. Greg was shouting. If it weren't for the little girl in his arms, he would be upstairs, putting himself between his sister and the asshole she called a husband.

"Goddammit, Loren, I provide you with everything and owe you nothing. I will be home when I get home. I did not marry you so you could turn into some kind of nagging wife. Now get a hold of yourself. I've got to get to work."

"Loren, I'm here."

"Oh, Riley, I'm sorry, I didn't hear you come in."

"Noelle let me in."

Riley heard heavy footsteps on the stairs.

He pulled Noelle closer and counted to ten . . . in Korean. He didn't really know Korean, but he'd taken Tae Kwon Do as a little boy and tried to remember counting. *Hana. Dul,* he thought about the hand movements that went with each number. Anything that would calm his temper and keep him from marching over and knocking the living shit out of his brother-in-law. By the time he reached *yeol,* Greg had left.

"I'll be right down. Just finishing my makeup."

"I'm going to fix some coffee, want some?" Riley hollered up to his sister. He didn't need any more coffee, but he did need something to distract himself.

"Sure."

Riley could hear the tears still bubbling in his baby sister's voice, but he'd wait until she came down to confront her.

After fixing two mugs, he set them onto the table and then made Noelle a bowl of cereal for breakfast.

"Daddy left." Noelle shoved a mouthful of Rice Krispies in.

"Yep, he sure did."

"I'm glad."

"Why is that?"

"He's always mad at me."

"He's not mad at you. He is just mad."

Noelle shook her head with force. "He gets mad at me. When he comes home, Mommy sends me to bed so he doesn't holler at me. If I wake up before him, I try to stay in my room or I come downstairs and eat my cereal. But I always stay quiet so he doesn't see me."

Yep, that did it. Riley officially wanted to murder Greg Delaney. Maybe he could find that bitch of a woman from this morning and introduce her to Greg. She could be his wife number two. That was, if he could ever persuade Loren to leave Greg.

What kind of man frightened his own daughter? Maybe he was biased, but Noelle was probably the sweetest, smartest kid in the world. She was definitely the prettiest.

"Is that mine?" Loren pointed to the extra mug and slid it over to herself.

"Yep. Take a seat. Noelle was just telling me about how her daddy doesn't like her and how she hides from him." Riley gave Loren a pointed look, letting her know that he expected details.

"Hey, No-No, would you like to eat your breakfast and watch television at the same time?"

Noelle didn't have to be asked twice, she was scooting out of her chair and sliding her bowl with her.

"Be careful, don't spill."

"I won't, Mommy."

When Noelle was out of earshot, Loren turned to Riley and began. "I want to leave Greg, and I need your help."

Chapter Three

ADELINE

he ladies frequented the Bougainvillea Country Club in their mission to keep up their facade of normal businesswomen. They wanted to be considered as nothing more than ladies who lunched and relaxed. They spent time nurturing the relationships with the other couples, families, and individuals who were privileged enough to be members of Bougainvillea. Well, privileged enough to be able to pay the bargain price of twenty-five thousand dollars a year for membership. Adeline always choked over the annual cost. For four unrelated women, all of adult age, that equaled four independent accounts. Sure, the club prided itself on its award-winning golf course, which stretched for six thousand four hundred twenty-one yards with an impressive par seventy.

Strolling into the country club restaurant they smiled, shook hands, and said hello to familiar faces. They tried to make meetings there a normal activity so that it didn't seem worthy of gossip when they were there. For Adeline, she made it a point to chat up everyone at the pool. She wasn't really interested in the actual activity so much as putting on her suit and looking hot as she lounged next to the pool with the attractive cabana boys. Melanie was the golf girl, and she felt it gave her an upper hand with the CEOs, since many of them ended up as enemies of the Iron Ladies. Sunday hung out on the tennis courts with her mean backhand smash, while Olivia seldom put down her camera, claiming to capture local flora and fauna. It didn't really help with their networking, but she was really stockpiling material that someday might come in handy.

"Hello, ladies, it's so nice to see you," Mr. Brown, the club manager, greeted them as they walked into the restaurant. "Miss Oakes, that was a great game you played against Mr. Bennett on the course."

"Thank you." Melanie stopped to talk to Mr. Brown while Adeline and Sunday moved on to find a seat, stopping seconds later when a weathered but kind face caught their attention.

Adeline allowed a genuine smile to tug at her lips. "Hi, Mrs. Sawyer, how are you feeling?"

"Oh, sweet girl, much better, thank you."

"Should you be eating that?" Sunday pointed to the chocolate lava cake on Mrs. Sawyer's plate. "I worry about your diabetes."

"If only my own children were as concerned about me as you four are."

"Do me a favor and only eat half, okay? I know it's hard to pass up but remember: moderation."

Mrs. Sawyer nodded.

When they were out of earshot Adeline stared at Sunday. "Really? Why stop her? The woman is in her seventies."

"Diabetes can kill her," Sunday defended.

"Yeah, what's it going to do, take ten years off her life? Newsflash, those ten years suck anyway. Let her have whatever the fuck she wants to have." Adeline threw her hands up into the air.

"Shhh," Melanie hissed as she caught up to them.

The four of them steered clear of Mr. Owens, who was the one member who took the rumor of them being call girls a bit too far and had actually tried to buy a date with Sunday. Olivia, Melanie, and Adeline had been merciless in their taunts after that one, since it had been Sunday who'd started the rumor in the first place.

"There she is." Olivia gave a chin nod toward the window, where she could see Loren coming up the walkway. "Way to go, look at her sexy-as-sin playmate. Yeah, I'd be divorcing that gouty ass wipe, too, if I could have a romp with him."

Adeline couldn't see the face of the man because he was wearing sunglasses and looking down but from this distance, she guessed he was a few inches over six feet, and with the sun shining down on him, she wasn't positive whether his hair was a dirty blond or just a light brown. Whatever it was, it worked for him.

"See what I mean? This case is going to garner too much attention for us, especially if she already has a dicksicle on the side."

"Adeline, don't be so crass." Melanie slapped Adeline's arm.

"If she's already having an affair, I understand Adeline's point though. Can't we just once have an easy client?"

"Easy?" Melanie scoffed. "I don't think there is such a thing."

"Just once I want someone to come to us, asking for help, only to tell us they've had the worst day of their life. I can hear it now, their ex got hit by a bus and they lost their job as a bus driver. Compared to some of these, shit, that would be easy."

The other three tried to fight the laughter since Loren

was getting closer and they wanted to come across as professional.

Loren wasn't able go five feet without stopping to say hello to someone. Her recognizable face and position in the community was too much publicity for Adeline's comfort. As she made her way closer to them, a pit in Adeline's stomach grew. The man hadn't looked her way yet, but there was something incredibly familiar about him.

"What's wrong with you?" Melanie gave her a worried look.

"Umm, I think I know him."

"Aww, shit, don't tell me that you've slept with him?"

"No . . . worse, I'm pretty sure I threatened to bury him."

Olivia choked on her water and coughed as she tried to clear her airway. In a haste to do something, Adeline bent and rummaged through her purse for something, anything. Sunglasses? She slid them on. Come on, come on, didn't she have a scarf or a ponytail holder? Of course, she didn't, because Adeline was in her uniform of the prim and proper Iron Lady who didn't use ponytail holders.

"Ow." Adeline jerked, and her head hit the table when Melanie kneed her in the forehead.

"Adeline, did you find what you were looking for? Loren is here." Melanie's voice sounded strained.

Adeline stuck her hand up and pointed her index finger. "One second." She slid her hand along the edge of the table until she felt it, aha, her napkin. She snagged it and brought it under the table with her. She was just starting to fold it into a bandana when a head popped under the table.

"Can I help you find whatever it is you're looking for?"

Adeline looked into the velvety brown eyes of the asshole from yesterday.

"No, I'm fine."

"You?" His tone was one-hundred percent aggravation but the smirk on his face was pure amusement.

Adeline wanted to smack that look right off. "You?" She pointed at him. "What? You can't even wait for her to get a divorce before you're sweeping in? You are just like all the other men who think they have standards, you're no different than those women who refuse to date guys who still live at home with their mother but have no problem dating a man that still lives at home with his wife. But you . . . you go after women who are still living with their husbands."

"Adeline." Melanie's tone was clipped. "Please come up here, we can hear you."

Adeline pulled back, tossed her sunglasses back into her purse, and then righted herself.

"Mrs. Delaney, what a pleasant surprise," Mrs. Sawyer interrupted. "I didn't know that you were a member here, it's such an honor."

Adeline used this little distraction to try to calm her nerves because fuck it all to hell the man was gorgeous and if he hadn't been such an uptight asshole the other day then she would have...ugh. She had no clue what she'd do because right now all she saw was pure infuriation.

"Oh, I'm just here to meet some friends." Loren stumbled over the lie.

Melanie interrupted, "If you'll excuse us, Mrs. Sawyer, we have a meeting with Mrs. Delaney."

"Oh, they're such nice ladies. How did you all meet? I had no clue the four of you were such good friends with the mayor's wife."

Sunday stood and placed a gentle hand on Mrs. Sawyer's shoulder. "Let me help you. Were you headed for your car or to the spa?" Sunday gently glided Mrs. Sawyer away from the table.

"She's good," Loren said, referring to Sunday's tactics.

Olivia nodded. "Yeah, she is. She's very diplomatic." Olivia turned those last words to Adeline like an accusation before smiling at Loren. "You seem to be quite the conversation starter. Is this the norm for you?"

"Unfortunately Greg has a lot of business associates, half of whom want to stay in his good graces and the other half want to get there. Most of them think that I'm the *in* they need."

"I see . . ." Adeline sincerely hoped that Melanie and Olivia were paying close attention, since Loren was saying exactly what she'd been trying to say all along. Since she walked in with the boy-toy-asshole, she was positive they needed to ditch her.

"It isn't gonna be a problem if someone reports seeing me with you ladies, will it?" Loren asked, looking around with a worried expression on her face. "I don't want to jeopardize the great work you ladies do."

"Not at all. No one here knows what we do, though, I have heard some very creative guesses," Sunday said as she slipped back into her seat.

"By the way, you didn't introduce your friend." Melanie held out her hand toward the man, but Adeline smacked Melanie's arm away.

"Oh, how rude of me, this is Riley Thomas, he's my brother."

Adeline coughed.

Riley nodded. "Nice to meet you. Loren has told me several things, but she obviously left some things out." He directed the last part at Adeline.

"I must have missed the last boat to Giveafuckistan." Adeline had intended to say it in a whisper, so only Olivia could hear her, but Olivia was never good at staying quiet. No, she had to laugh out loud. Adeline stomped her foot on top of Livi's.

"Ouch." Olivia pulled her foot away from Adeline's heel.

"Shhh." Melanie glared at both Adeline and Olivia.

"I hope you don't mind, but Riley wanted to come along to offer his support," Loren's tone clearly implied that she was needing the moral support that he offered her.

Riley groaned.

She gave her brother the *mom stare*.

What? Riley mouthed.

"Well, it looks like Adeline and Riley know each other." Sunday smiled and gave Adeline a wink. No one else got to respond, because a waiter in a tuxedo with the Bougainvillea emblem embroidered on his lapel came up to the table.

"Membership number for the account please."

Adeline recited. "Two-six-one-three. Add it all to my account, please." Each member had their own number, and one of the many rules of Bougainvillea was that you had to spend a minimum of five hundred per month at the club or the amount was added to your membership fees. The girls elected to spend it in the restaurant.

"I'll have a hamburger, medium," Melanie said. "Loren? Riley?"

"Just a glass of ice water with lemon please." Adeline arched a brow. "Just water? The menu is right in front of you." She handed it over to Loren, who passed it to her brother.

"Just a cup of coffee, black." Riley set the menu aside. "I hate when people ruin coffee with all that other shit."

The waiter turned to Adeline. "Just a coffee for me, but I'd like whipped cream, milk, half and half, stevia, and bring some real sugar just in case I change my mind. Oh, and some cinnamon." Adeline matched Riley's tone. "I'm not a fan of plain and bitter."

The water glasses splashed as Sunday and Melanie moved their legs to kick Adeline. Olivia was busy coughing and Loren's eyes were wide as saucers.

Riley was in a stare-off with Adeline.

"Well, I'll have the chicken salad sandwich please." Sunday handed the menu over to the waiter.

"I'll have the same." Olivia pointed to Sunday, and they both cracked up laughing.

When the waiter left, Melanie scanned the nearby area. "I'm not sure what the hell is going on, but I'm going to ignore you two. Loren, we've decided to take on your case." She met Adeline's stare.

The relief that washed over Loren could be felt by everyone. Riley looked at his sister with love and affection, but he didn't exactly look impressed with the ladies.

Melanie continued, "Considering you're here, I take it you were made aware of our retainer fee."

Loren eyed Riley, and he nodded. "That is another reason my brother is here, he has offered to pay the fee for me."

At least he's generous somewhere, Adeline mouthed, her face tilted away so no one actually noticed.

"Okay. But it isn't quite that simple. You'll find that we work . . . how shall I say this, differently."

"Differently?" Riley was no longer focused on just Adeline, but on all of them.

Adeline hated the fact that something about his voice resonated with her and sent shivers down her spine. Melanie, ever observant, gave Adeline a questioning look, but all talk had to pause when the waiter returned with their food.

"Such wonderful service, and it's fast, too," Loren observed.

"It's how they compensate for ridiculous membership fees," Olivia said before she took a bite of her sandwich.

With his cup of coffee in his hands, Riley locked eyes with Melanie. "Care to explain, exactly how do you work differently? Do you bury them?" He asked the last question of Adeline.

"Um, well, no we don't bury anyone. I'll let you and Adeline handle that. We go above and beyond. We do whatever is needed. Loren doesn't want to have to worry about money once she divorces, but she also doesn't want to worry about retaliation. That's our job. We make sure that we get enough evidence, so your sister can sleep peacefully at night. We do that by not ruining Greg or his reputation."

"Why not? We should get the evidence and release it to the media, let everyone know the type of man that he is."

"If we destroy Greg, what will he have left? Nothing. He's a loose cannon. No one wants an enemy who has nothing left to lose. We want him to let her walk away and live in peace. Once Loren and Greg are divorced and we close this case, Loren will always be our client in regard to this case. This is a commitment to Loren that we will hold everything that we discover and have it available for her until she remarries, or Noelle is eighteen years of age."

"Shit." Adeline interrupted as she spilled the hot coffee on her shirt.

"Adeline . . ." Melanie chided her, but Riley grabbed a napkin from the table and dabbed the spot on Adeline's shirt, as if he were afraid she burned herself. There was an awkward silence as everyone watched. Adeline tried to take the napkin from Riley, but he refused, giving her his dashing smile as he continued to pat away at the spot . . . on Adeline's breasts. Unwilling to be groped in public, no matter how hot the groper was, Adeline snatched the napkin away from him and gave him a pointed glare.

"I'm sure all that shit you added stains."

"Awkward," Sunday murmured.

And it was, so Adeline cleared her throat and picked up where Melanie left off.

"We'll also get Loren a huge settlement. Oh, and by the time we're done, your husband will be begging you to stay."

Adeline winked at Loren. "But you won't give him the time of day."

Loren giggled.

"Now, if that sounds like something you're up for, here is a list of things we need from you." Adeline slid a piece of paper in front of Loren but kept her hand firmly on it. Loren was meant to read the paper but not take it. The ladies didn't want any evidence getting out. They needed a list of places that Greg liked to frequent, and the woman, or women, she suspected that he might be having an affair with. They also needed copies of their prenuptial agreement, the last two years of phone records, any information that she could think of that might be pertinent, like their internet provider and common passwords used by Greg. Finally, Loren had to make a list of Greg's favorite possessions. "Commit this list to memory so you can start gathering the items, and then Sunday will be in contact with you," Adeline said as way of stating that the meeting was over. "Wait for her text, it will be coded. Take the first letter of each word to solve it. We always meet at our office."

"Care to explain?" Melanie asked once Loren and Riley were gone.

"You know how Olivia runs every morning?"

Melanie nodded.

"You know why she runs every morning?"

Olivia interrupted. "It's my guarantee that the day can't get any worse since a run is well...fucking horrid."

"Exactly." Adeline tapped the tip of her nose. "Well, this is why I don't run, because assholes like Riley Thomas only prove that your day can always get worse."

Chapter Four

ADELINE

$\mathcal{T}$he next morning, Sunday sent Loren a message that looked as if it had come from some garden club.

UNKNOWN: Ivy Roses Of Nature Lillies and Dahlias In Excess Supply Orange Friendly Finches In Cages Evaluated. Ten Available Maybe.

*IRON LADIES OFFICE, **ten AM.***

BY NINE THIRTY, the Iron Ladies were set up in the conference room, waiting for Loren as they continued to dig into whatever they could find. They were also organizing the tasks that they'd be responsible for once they put operation Take Down Greg Delaney into motion, which was something they all got a thrill from.

What made their team invincible was that each one possessed a skill that was beneficial to their clients and to their company.

Adeline was a roadster, a master at tactical driving and, as such, she could tail any subject without being seen. The bad side was she considered it very boring, especially if the subject never broke the fucking speed limit. Since she wasn't exactly known for her patience, the busy Orlando traffic, cars constantly cutting her off and making her swerve, was not her cup of tea. When she focused on her goal of staying invincible and not attracting any attention to herself, then Adeline was a regular Houdini on four wheels.

Melanie was the negotiator, the MacGyver of the group. Whether they needed a smooth talker or lock picker, Melanie had the skills.

Sunday was the group hacker, originally a software engineering major before switching to criminal justice. She could hack any system and reroute their security before anyone realized they had a breach.

Olivia was the sharpshooter. True, she was the Annie Oakley of the group, but Olivia was also the Ansel Adams and always had her camera handy.

When the elevator opened and Loren Delaney and Riley stepped off, Melanie waved them over to the boardroom, where they all sat with notepads.

"Welcome. Can I get you some coffee or water?" Adeline stood and moved to the coffee maker to fix herself a cup. She had made a vow that, today, Riley Thomas wasn't going to get under her skin.

"No, thank you," Loren answered.

"I'm good, thanks," Riley replied.

Adeline let out a small chuckle and set a cup in front of Riley anyway, already ruining her promise. She had made his cup the way she liked hers, with stevia and one cream. They locked eyes, he had started to glare at her, but the challenge in her eyes had him laughing instead.

She swung into her seat and inwardly groaned oh, the things women do to garner attention.

"First things first," Melanie said to start the meeting, and everyone took a seat. "Does anyone know that you've come to see us today?"

"Nope, just Riley." Loren patted her brother's arm. "Noelle goes to preschool today anyway, so it worked out great."

"No interview-starved reporters?" Sunday asked as she scanned the internet to see if there were any breaking stories or gossip about Loren Delaney.

"I promise you, no one."

"Good, let's keep it that way. The last thing we need is for your husband to find out you're digging and start being more careful about whatever he's doing," Melanie mumbled.

"Oh, I'm positive that Greg doesn't suspect a thing." Loren let out a long, drawn-out sigh. "Why should he? I'm only a woman, and he's a powerful man who controls me and is so much wiser." Loren let out a disgusted laugh. "The last thing Greg has ever done is worry about me or my where-abouts, as long as I'm not embarrassing him, he hardly remembers I exist."

"What's that saying? When you least it expect it?" Sunday looked over the lid of her laptop and gave a wicked smile to Loren. "It is so much better when they don't see it coming. It means that they aren't trying nearly as hard to hide their tracks."

Loren nodded in agreement.

Melanie steepled her index fingers. "Now, my second question is, did you bring all your electronic devices along?"

"Yes, two cell phones and my iPad."

"Can you pass them to Sunday, please? We need to make sure there's no spy software installed."

Sunday took them and began the scan.

"So, what's the next step? Are you going to trail Greg's every move or hack into his camera feed and get the info? Isn't that what computer gurus do?"

"Loren . . . don't believe everything you see on television. None of those things are as easy as they make them appear. We will be carrying on two different investigations. The first is to prove he's having an affair, and the second is to get whatever dirt we can on him so he will stay quiet and accommodating during and after the divorce. Hacking into his systems and recording him is inadmissible in court, and it's illegal. I know you want custody of your daughter, but that won't happen if you're in jail."

"Plus, no one looks good in orange," Adeline added. What she didn't add was that they would be hacking into his computers, his cell phones, and his security footage. They'd do whatever they needed to get the dirt; they just didn't openly talk about it.

"Got it. So where do we start?" Loren asked.

"We start with surveillance. We want to see where he goes, who he hangs out with, and what he's doing when he thinks no one else is watching." Melanie pointed to each line item on her list as she read them off. "More or less, we need to catch him with his pants down . . . literally."

Adeline flipped open her notebook, she had some questions she had compiled last night while scrolling through LinkedIn and searching for anyone who referenced working in the mayor of Orlando's office within the past five years. Adeline came to the first woman: Ely York, she was an attractive brunette, twenty-two years old. The next name, Eva

Wolfe, she was a sexy brunette, twenty-three years old. Adeline continued searching and found Sienna Miller, Mia Snow, Deena Charles, and Jessa Christoferson. All of them were brunettes, all of them were endowed in the chest, and all of them were nothing like the tiny blonde sitting across from her.

Adeline felt sorry for Loren, truly she did, but she had discovered a long time ago that not everyone was going to like her, case in point, her own parents. Adeline would rather be upfront with Loren than worry about whether Loren still liked her.

"What can you tell us about these interns?"

Adeline slid the list of names to Loren, and the other woman scanned them, tiny frown lines creasing her forehead as she did.

"Not much, really. I know that he offers internships to students from the University of Central Florida who are getting their degree in political science. The internships are for two years. I usually meet them at some point, but I don't ever get to truly know them."

Adeline leaned forward, using her pen to indicate the top three names on the list. "You don't remember anything about these three women?"

"I know that she worked for Greg a few years ago."

"And this one?" Adeline pointed to the next name, Sienna.

"I don't remember her."

"Well, she started at city hall about four months ago, and since the program runs for two years, I would assume she's still there."

"How about Mia, Jessa, or Eva?"

"I only met them in passing and they all seemed lovely. What are you trying to tell me?"

"I'm not trying to tell you anything, but I am trying to

find out why all of these women all fit the same physical profile."

Loren gulped and then scratched the side of her head. "I don't know. I just never thought about what these women looked like. This is making me feel like I've been an idiot all along."

"We don't want you to blame yourself. We are trying to find patterns and we are trying to see what you've picked up on. Sometimes wives have had suspicions about their husbands but they've just never said them out loud. If that's the case, then now is the time to get it all out."

"No, there's nothing."

Adeline pulled back on her questioning because Loren was starting to look ganged up on. "Olivia, do you have any questions?"

"Loren, what can you tell us about your husband's golf activities?"

"He plays almost every day at the Winter Park Golf and Racquet Club, that's where we are members."

"Do you know who he usually plays with?"

"He meets a few friends, usually other councilmen."

"Did you make a list of his favorite hangouts and people he might be seen with?"

Loren reached into her purse and pulled out several sheets of paper before handing them to Olivia. "This is everyone I could think of and all the places, including restaurants where he holds lunch meetings."

"Perfect." Olivia perused the list, then handed it to Sunday so she could scan it into the computer and send them all a copy.

"Did you bring a copy of your prenup?" Loren handed over the copy to Melanie. "We'll send this over to Barrett Huxley. He's our attorney and will keep all of it confidential, I promise you."

The Iron Ladies kept him on retainer. They'd all met in college and together they'd built their businesses. Barrett had quickly become a respected attorney. Not only did he help them decipher the legal documents, but also he helped the clients when needed. Once the ladies had completed their surveillance operation, they'd hand their clients and all of the collected evidence over to Barrett, who then assisted each woman with the legal process and settlement negotiations. Maybe it was because the ladies were so good at collecting evidence that Barrett had never lost a case.

"I'm not worried about him, but what about other people in his firm? Greg is an attorney, or was before he was elected. They all stick together."

"Don't worry, we have a private email server between the two of us, so not even his secretary knows." Sunday tapped her fingers on the table.

"Finally, did you bring a list of his favorite possessions?" Adeline waited for the list.

"I was kind of stumped when you said things that he likes most, do you mean like his status in the community or the gold ingots his father left him?"

Adeline laughed. "Well, I was thinking more along the lines of family heirlooms and less along the lines of traceable gold pieces."

"Oh, then that would be his Maybach. Umm . . . his golf clubs. Probably his Rolex? I'm not really sure."

"Well, since he drives his Maybach daily, that might be difficult. So I'd say his Rolex or his golf clubs."

"Rolex or golf clubs for what?" Loren glanced between Adeline, Melanie, Olivia, and Sunday to see who'd give the answer, but the ladies were busy having a silent conversation.

"The item that you're going to pawn."

Riley let out a groan. "Are you fucking kidding me? That is the most asinine thing that I've ever heard of. Can't you think of something a little more . . . ummm . . . I don't know, job appropriate? This isn't an episode of fucking *Pawn Stars*."

"Riley, shhh," Loren reprimanded.

"What? This is ridiculous. This is what fifteen thousand dollars is going to?"

Adeline stood and placed both hands on her hips. "First of all, we aren't here for you."

"No, just my money."

"Your opinion will never pay our bills. Sunday, give Mr. Thomas back his money and show them to the elevator. We have a waiting list. When Loren is begging for visitation to see her daughter and has no one to blame but her brother, then maybe he'll stop scratching his balls long enough to realize that he has no one to blame except himself for the way their lives turned out."

"Please don't. I need you. I know what you can do. I know what you did for Mrs. Kletcher. Please. Give Riley back his money. I'll come up with it on my own by tomorrow, I promise. I can't lose my daughter, she's all I have in this world."

"You have me." Riley's voice was gruff.

"Obviously she doesn't think so, since you're willing to throw her and her daughter to the wolves." Adeline was fuming. "The fact is, Mr. Thomas, you seem to have a bad case of diarrhea of the mouth. You say things without thinking about those around you. Let me tell you what you and your self-centered, cocky-ass, big-mouth attitude has cost your sister. You see other investigators are going to go out with their buddies and brag to one another about being the one to land the case to try and catch Greg, or they will give him a heads up because let's face it, you all don't know when to keep your mouths shut. But we don't do that. No, we'll be too busy working, or should I say, would have been too busy working getting Loren every single penny she wanted. We aren't just private investigators, we are coaches. We work to help women regain the confidence that asshole men try and strip from them. We work together with our clients so that they are confident and strong enough to face their demons and are truly ready to live a life as a single person. We don't do the bare minimum to get the job done, then leave our clients hanging. No. We stand with them as a team. Because it is one thing to face an angry woman, it is an entirely different thing to face a bunch of angry women. Oh wait, I'm sure you can tell us exactly how that feels Mr. Thomas, look around and tell me, how do you feel now?"

"Please Adeline, don't. I need you all." Loren's words were muffled with tears.

Riley grabbed his sister's hand but she ripped it from his grip. "I'll give you however much you need, you know that. Please stop crying."

Adeline interrupted. "Mr. Thomas, I don't want to do business with you. You can take your money and shove it—"

"Shhh." Melanie smacked Adeline's leg, trying to reel her in.

Loren stared at her brother. "I love you but right now I need your support. If you can't support me without constantly doubting what I'm doing, then I need to avoid you until this is over. I've got to do this. It's for Noelle. If it was just me, I'd put up with it."

"He treats you like a dog, you can't stay."

"Then why are you giving the women who can help me such a hard time?"

Adeline sat back down, because she knew that Loren had just won, but never being the type of person that could leave well enough alone, she had to dig one more time. "Mr. Thomas, would you still like your money back?"

"No."

"I'm sorry, could you speak a little louder?"

"Adeline," Melanie, Olivia, and Sunday all said in exasperation.

Adeline turned and faced them then gave a cheeky wink.

"Then as I was saying, decide which item you want to pawn, and we'll all meet at Queen's Gold. This is one time you won't want to bring your brother. Coco, well, she and he won't exactly get along."

"Fine, but I still don't see the point in pawning something."

"I want you to really think about this and answer truthfully. Have you ever gotten so angry that you did something crazy . . . like broke something or hit something? Maybe you threw a Waterford goblet, I don't know, something, anything."

Loren let out a little groan.

"Ah ha, you have. What'd you do?" Adeline circled her index finger.

"When I was in high school, I was waiting to turn into a parking spot. The place was crowded, there were no spots. So I'd been waiting for this spot a good ten minutes, just as the car backed out and I started to pull in, a little Sportster coming from the other direction swooped in and took the spot. The woman just got out of her little convertible, flipped me the middle finger, and walked off. I was pissed and had to circle several more times before I found a spot. When I got out of my car, I grabbed my purse and my milkshake—"

"Oh, god," Adeline moaned, already imagining where this was going.

"As I walked past the girl's car, I *accidentally* dropped my milkshake inside, but the lid wasn't on all the way, oops. Dairy in the Florida sun sucks big time. Of course, I didn't realize how bad until I had Noelle and she dropped a bottle of milk that I didn't see for a few days."

"That is priceless. Can I ask you how that made you feel afterward?"

"Vindicated." Loren's words were spoken with conviction.

"Did you ever regret doing it?"

"Sad to say, no, not once. That woman really was a bitch."

"This is why we have you do this, it seems trivial, I know. But it's the first step of moving on, and you need to feel that your actions are justifiable. And you need a little bit of absolution from a few retaliative actions."

Riley sat there shaking his head, obviously never having heard this story or seeing this side of his sister.

Melanie was still laughing while Adeline and Riley were in a stare down . . . again. "Okay, well, I think we have everything we need for today. We'll be in touch." She stood and shook Loren's hand.

Riley stopped and turned to face Adeline, a slow heat crept up her cheeks. "Tell me, do you actually do anything that requires talent? You know, besides being a pain in the ass?"

An evil smile crossed Adeline's face. "I'll make a deal with you."

"What?" Riley didn't look pleased.

"What's something that you want, really want?" Adeline arched one brow.

"Besides seeing you knocked off your fucking high horse? I don't know."

Adeline tapped her toe and waited.

"Fine, I want to get approved for rezoning on a piece of land that I purchased so I can build affordable housing."

Adeline held out her hand. "Let me show you a little about my job, and I'll help you get your property rezoned."

Riley was slow to move, but finally, he took her hand in his and shook, instantly appearing as if he regretted it when triumph flashed in Adeline's eyes.

Adeline left the office bouncing. Fucking *bouncing*. She felt as if she'd just gotten the upper hand on Riley Thomas. She may not have a lot of good qualities, she knew that she could be selfish and a bitch at times, but damn it all to hell, she was a kickass roadster. She could manipulate a car better than she could . . . Riley. Adeline let out a laugh and then silently chastised herself for being a grade-A bitch, again.

Chapter Five

ADELINE

he one thing that was awesome about Adeline's co-workers was that they each knew what to do. Sure, they talked things out, but during the day, they went their own ways and did their individual jobs. It worked really well for them.

Adeline had taken what she had learned about the interns and then set to trying to discover more about them on other social media sites. From searching Facebook and Instagram she quickly learned that besides their looks the other common denominator seemed to be location, location, location. They all had taken food shots and tagged it Capital Grille. Since there were only two Capital Grilles, Adeline decided to give them both a go, and headed to the one on International Drive first.

Adeline shimmied her shoulders then ran her hands under her breasts to make sure that the girls were nice and perky. If she were ever asked to write her memoirs, people would crucify her over the stunts she had pulled all in the name of getting an insider tip. Strutting up to the bar, she bent down to check the buckle on her strappy stilettos, confident that this gave the man pouring the alcohol a hint of her generous cleavage.

"What can I do for you?" His voice was smooth as he set a napkin onto the bar in front of her.

"What can you do for me or what can you get me? That might be two different things." Adeline winked as she trailed one devilishly red painted fingernail along the polished surface. "As far as drinks, I'll take a vodka cranberry with a twist of lime. Top shelf, please."

"Coming right up." The bartended grabbed the more expensive vodka off the shelf. "So, what is a beautiful lady like you doing here all alone?"

Adeline stuck out her bottom lip and pouted. "Would you believe me if I told you that I was stood up?"

"What kind of idiot would stand up a gorgeous woman like you?"

"You're too kind. Someone who I thought was genuinely a nice guy but clearly wasn't. He's going through a divorce, maybe he decided that he just wasn't ready to start dating, or that he wanted to stay with his wife, you know? Which, if that's the case, then good for him. I mean, I would never want to stand between a man and true love or hinder a couple from trying one more time." Adeline drew out the long *I* sound to make her words sound a little more Southern. "I want more for myself. I'm not one who would be happy being the other woman."

"Well, if he did stand you up, then it is his loss because, honey, I'd never stand you up. By the way, did you leave your name with the hostess in case he shows up, maybe he's just running late?"

Adeline picked up her phone and touched the screen to check the time. Amping up her act, she let out a long, drawn-out sigh. "I did, but I doubt he's coming. He said that he'd meet me in the bar forty-five minutes ago."

"You know there are two Capital Grille locations. Maybe he's at the other one."

Adeline let out a small chuckle and then placed her hands on the bartender's as he set her drink in front of her. "Thank you, that's sweet of you to try to make me feel better, but he said he comes here all of the time, and he gave me the directions, so I know this is the right place."

"Who was it you were meeting, maybe I know him?"

Adeline leaned in to whisper. "Greg Delaney."

The bartender's eyes widened in shock, then he stuck out his hand. "I'm Greyson."

"Hi, Greyson, I'm Adeline."

"Adeline, I hate to tell you this, but since you told me you don't date married men, I feel it's only right to help you, especially since I have four sisters. Greg Delaney isn't leaving his wife, in fact, he and his wife were here last night. I mean, he comes here with a lot of different people, and yes, some of them are beautiful women, but he and his wife didn't look as if they were on the outs."

"But he's the mayor. Why would he lie? Don't people realize that he's cheating on his wife?" Adeline wiped at her face to smooth away her crocodile tears. "My soulmate is not another woman's husband. No, thank you, that is not me."

"He's usually here on Tuesdays and Thursdays, they're our slowest nights, and he sits over in that side room, so most people never see him." Greyson fixed a drink for another person before making his way back over to Adeline.

But she had laid a twenty next to her half-empty glass and was already out the door. Adeline would have to send Olivia back there on Tuesdays and Thursdays to snag a slew of pictures.

When Adeline finally got home, she headed to her bedroom. Part of the company uniform was wearing dresses and heels to give that polished-lady look. But at home, they let loose, let their real character shine. In a pair of hip-hugging jeans, Adeline headed to the kitchen and grabbed the bottle of Beluga vodka to continue where she'd left off earlier. Melanie jumped up from the couch and grabbed four glasses while Olivia snagged the orange juice and cranberry juice. Then they all settled in the living room, where Sunday was lounging, attention riveted to whatever she was working on.

"Olivia, can you start swinging by Capital Grille on International Drive on Tuesday and Thursday? There is a small room that I assume is used for parties on the other side of the bar, look in there."

"Will do. Am I looking for anything in particular?"

"Just a tip that Greg likes to hang out there on those days with different women that aren't his wife."

Melanie raised one brow but didn't ask how Adeline got that information.

"Got it." Olivia nodded before taking a sip of her drink. "So, are you and Riley going to be a problem? Because, I have to tell you, if you don't get whatever feud you two have between you under control, it's going to cause issues."

"Nope. He's going to cave."

"Oh, god, Adeline, what did you do?"

"Nothing. Well . . . just made a deal with him. I agreed to help him with one of his projects if he spends a day in my shoes. Not literally, of course. But I am going to take him to Zotz."

"Fuck, we better bring the paramedics." Melanie shook her head.

"And vomit bags, remember the first time we all rode with Adeline on the open road? Imagine on a closed circuit." Sunday let out a groan and held her stomach.

"I'll pick up a neck brace in case he gets whiplash," Olivia said before taking another, longer sip of her drink.

"Did you not get the hint that you drive like a maniac

when even Siri changed your GPS directions and said, 'Stop, you've arrived at your destination, now let me the fuck out?'" Everyone except Adeline gave Sunday a high-five for that comment.

"Haha, very funny. I'm just tired of his cocky attitude. Thinking that we need his money and then freaking his poor sister out. What a douche."

"When Loren started crying, I saw something in him, it changed." Sunday nodded.

"I saw something in him, too . . . oh, wait, that was in his jeans." Adeline laughed and then ducked when Melanie swung a pillow at her head.

"Really? You can hate him and admire his crotch at the same time?"

"I'm multi-talented, what can I say?" Adeline shrugged. "Do you think after all of this that Loren will go back to her husband? Sunday? What do you think?"

Sunday was still fixated on her laptop when she answered, "Umm, I agree, Adeline is multi-talented."

"Will you three grow up? I meant about Loren backing out."

"No, I don't think she will back out." Sunday didn't look up from her computer as she made that announcement.

"Sunday, what are you looking for? I swear, you spend more than half your life behind that computer screen." Adeline pointed. "You're going to get a hump in your back and then never find a hot guy."

"Who says that I'm looking?"

"You can't avoid men forever," Adeline singsonged.

Sunday looked up from her laptop. "Oh, believe me, I can. By the way, you all need to see this."

"What?" The ladies moved to stand behind Sunday and read over her shoulder.

"The mayor has a few land deals coming up, and one is

rather large, one of the largest investments the city has made since the budget cuts. I'm trying to get more information on it because the property isn't slated for anything; it is just being purchased."

"Who owns the property?" Adeline asked, thoroughly curious.

"That's what is pissing me off, I don't know. All the records are sealed. Kind of like what Loren mentioned . . . hidden."

"Do you think he's selling her property to the city?"

"Don't know." Sunday closed the screen she was on and opened another one.

"Can he do that? If it is Loren's, was hers before the marriage, and is slated for Noelle's trust, then technically he committed fraud, right?" Adeline looked at Melanie for answers.

"It depends." Melanie picked up her iPad and started Googling.

"On what?"

"On how the trust was set up, who the trustees are. But we aren't even positive that the property Sunday found is Loren's. Does Belle still work at the courthouse?"

"Yep, I just saw her the other day at Starbucks. She is doing great and happy that we were able to help her get rid of her crazy ex."

"She find anyone new yet?"

"Nah, she says all the guys nowadays send dick pics. She's waiting for one to send her a picture of his latest paycheck and the inside of his medicine cabinet. Until then, she won't know whether he has a stable job, or what kind of fucked-up shit he has going on. She thinks those two things should be prerequisites."

"Word." Sunday held up her glass in solidarity.

"Have you been able to find anything, Livi?" Adeline

stepped back and then moved back over to the sofa to take her seat again.

"Yes, thought you'd never ask." Olivia set down her drink then pulled out three stacks of black-and-white photographs from the folder in front of her. She handed Melanie, Sunday, and Adeline each a set. "As you know, I've been hanging out at City Hall, and, well, it's been boring as fuck until today. Our good Mr. Mayor left to go play golf, but when he arrived at the Winter Park Golf and Racquet Club, he didn't grab his clubs."

"He didn't? What did he do?" Adeline asked, already flipping through the photos.

"He got into a silver Mercedes with dark tinted windows and left."

"Where did they go?" Adeline flipped through the photos and stared at a small brick home.

"To a home over in Isle Wood off Snow Queen. Unfortunately, I have no clue who she is, do any of you?" Olivia pulled off a piece of paper and handed it to Sunday. "This is the license plate number and the address on Snow Queen, see what you can find out, please."

"On it." Sunday refocused on her keyboard. "I sent Piper a text with the license plate number to see if she could find out anything for us."

"Good to have deputies as friends." Adeline held her glass out and tapped it against Sunday's.

Melanie hadn't said a word, she was still staring at the photos.

"You're awfully quiet, what's up?"

"This woman, she looks familiar." Melanie took a snapshot of the photo with her iPad then uploaded it to several different image-recognition programs, including TinEye, CamFind, and Google Visual Search. A second later, she let out a low whistle. "Oh, shit. I knew she was familiar." Melanie pulled her legs up under her and sat taller on the couch. "The woman is . . . Hillary Chatham."

"Holy fuck." Adeline spewed her vodka. "As in Councilman Chatham's wife?"

"That's the one."

"Is that their house?" Adeline was wiping up the mess she'd made.

"Not sure, the home isn't listed in the tax records."

"Okay, we don't know whose home it is, nor whether something inappropriate is going on, right? All these pictures are pretty innocent."

"Well, from what I've gathered, no one has ever accused him of having an affair, the man is spotless." Sunday opened a document on her computer. "Gregory William Delaney, graduated valedictorian from Boone High School, received his master's degree from Stetson in business, and according to all interviews, he married the love of his life . . ."

Melanie scoffed at that remark.

Sunday smiled and continued. "He has one daughter, Noelle, and no criminal record . . . not even a fucking traffic citation. He won the race for mayor by a landslide, and he is known for his benevolent altruism and good intentions of increasing the wellbeing of mankind."

"Whoa." Olivia could not hide her surprise. "I think someone just dropped a pound of bullshit over here."

Sunday stifled a laugh and resumed. "He also supports a handful of charities and appears to be transparent in his actions. Should I go on, or do you all have the hang of it? Publicly, Greg Delaney is the golden boy. All-American good guy."

"The hell he is, Greg Delaney sounds like someone who has taken a lot of time and spent a lot of money to carve a good reputation for himself." Melanie scoffed again. "Just remember that Ted Bundy was considered an all-American golden boy as well."

"Scary thing is, he sounds like someone I'd vote for a second time." Adeline shook her head, obviously distraught by that thought.

Olivia shrugged. "So, he's smart and knows how to cover his ass. No surprises there."

"Or, he has the money to hire smart people," Sunday added.

"Sunday, can you send a message to Loren and let her know we are going to go see Coco and then I'm going to take her brother for the ride of his life."

Everyone laughed at Adeline's remark.

"No double entendre there." Adeline winked, then got up and headed back to her room.

That night she had a hard time falling asleep. She tried counting sheep, but those fluffy fuckers weren't having it. She had so much on her mind, and it all had to do with Riley Thomas. She had no clue why he got under her skin. But all she could focus on was his chiseled jaw, his crooked smile, and his strong hands. She hadn't had sex in over a year, which was both sad and frustrating.

Even if she hadn't been neck-deep in a dry spell, she still would have thought the man was fucking hot. Too bad the Iron Ladies had a code of ethics because, if they didn't, she would have been all over him. But he was an uptight asshole who hated her music.

Guys like him didn't go for girls like her. Sure, she was voluptuous and curvy, but she likened herself to a fancy sports car. Most men wanted sports cars, but they bought family cars in the long run. Adeline was all sports car.

Chapter Six

ADELINE

$\mathcal{A}$deline sat in the back parking lot of Queen's Gold pawn shop. She was seriously shocked that she was the first to arrive, but she didn't have to wait long because within five minutes, Melanie, Olivia, and Sunday had all pulled in, followed by Loren.

Adeline let out a sigh, because Loren had listened and left her brother at home.

"Are we ready?" Olivia clapped her hands. "Coco is expecting us." Queen's Gold wasn't in the most prestigious location: it was nestled in the middle of Orlando's red-light district. From prostitution, to drug deals, if you wanted to buy something illegal, it could all be done in this area, and the funny part was, it was all within a few-block radius of the Orlando Police Department headquarters and the Orange County Sheriff's Department's main office. Not to mention Orlando City Hall and the Federal Courthouse.

Queen's Gold had wrought-iron bars on the windows and doors.

Olivia grabbed the golf clubs from the back of Loren's

SUV before Loren locked up, and then they all headed across the parking lot.

"Who's that?" Loren whispered, her voice sounding as if she was scared to death.

"That's Coco, come on." Adeline walked up and gave Coco a wide smile.

"I know that you want to hug me, don't you? Come on, Coco, admit it?"

"Girl, if I do what I want to do with you, I'll be back in prison. Now get yo ass inside."

"Loren, this is Coco. Coco, this is your next charge." Coco folded her arms and scanned Loren up and down. "Don't be like that. Loren, don't let her scare you. She's like a dark chocolate Milky Way candy bar."

Coco spread her legs shoulder width apart and glared, then let out a quiet laugh. Contrary to what anyone would expect, it wasn't a boom befitting such a large woman, it was high-pitched and girly. Loren couldn't help it. Coco's laugh was contagious.

"Yep, she likes to pretend that she's hard. She isn't."

"Get your asses inside before I beat the shit out of all of you. I'm just getting ready to eat breakfast, got my hominy and honey all ready. You five best be hungry."

"Yum." Melanie rubbed her stomach.

"Hominy, what?" Loren looked confused.

"Coco likes to be weird. She says that's what they call it in her country, but it's plain old grits." Adeline winked at Loren.

"Where's she from?"

"Tonga."

Once they were all inside, Coco locked back up before leading everyone upstairs. "Eat, then we will talk business," Coco ordered, dishing each one a bowl of hominy with a mound of honey poured in the middle.

The place was quiet as everyone did as they were told.

Only once Coco was done did she turn to Loren, saying, "So, tell me about you. You have a man not treating you right?"

Loren nodded. "Yeah. You could say that."

"Of course I could, I just did. What is he doing?"

Loren glanced left then right, trying to see what the ladies had to say about being questioned.

"What you looking at girl, don't you know what he's done, or are you just wanting to divorce him for the hell of it? Not that I blame you, most men get on my nerves too."

"He's been lying to me, cheating on me, god, what isn't he doing? His own daughter is scared to death of him."

"Has he put a hand on your daughter?"

Loren shook her head. "No. It's just that he always screams at her and me. Noelle hides from him."

"Girl, you're much too young to be worrying about husband problems like that."

Adeline lightly squeezed Loren's hand to infuse her with a bit of strength. Loren blinked, trying to hold back the tears as she ate, and Coco turned her attention to the rest of them.

"So any of you ladies get stupid lately? Do I need to whip some common sense into you all?"

They all laughed. This was Coco's way of asking whether they had a man in their lives.

"Nope," Sunday answered. "And I don't want one. More headaches than they are worth. Learned that the hard way."

Coco made a clicking sound with her tongue. "You always were a smart one."

"How about you, Olivia?"

"Not me."

"Melanie?"

"Nope."

"Adeline?"

"Not me." Melanie, Olivia, and Sunday laughed like a couple of preteens with a secret. "Will you three stop already?" Adeline snapped, then she shoved her last spoonful of grits and honey into her mouth and stood. "Well, it looks like we're all done, why don't we head downstairs to look at the clubs?"

"Don't disappoint me, Adeline. Don't get fooled by the one-eyed wizard," Coco said, leaving the others fighting back their laughs as she dropped her bowl into the sink. The others, realizing the conversation was obviously over, followed suit before heading downstairs.

"Hand me that nine iron, would you?" Loren slid it out and handed it over. "Honma golf clubs, don't get these in here very often. Your dirtbag husband a pro golfer?"

"No, he's a showoff."

"Oh, one of those." Coco moved from behind her counter and over to the bag to examine it closer. "He doesn't play a lot, does he?"

"No, he plays all the time. Every day."

Coco titled her head, confused since the gold clubs showed very little wear. But Adeline caught Coco's attention and gave an infinitesimal shake of her head. Leaning over, Adeline whispered, sotto voce, "Depends who you ask. Ask him, and he'll tell you that he's golfing all the time, ask Olivia's camera and it'll show him going to the golf course to meet women and then leaving with them."

Coco leaned back on her heels and looked up to meet Adeline's eyes. The only person probably more jaded than Adeline was Coco. Pawnshops were sad places full of people's broken dreams and promises. But Coco hated seeing anyone shit on.

"How much are you looking to get out of these?"

"I have no clue. I don't know what he paid for them."

"Mm-hmm. I'll give you five thousand, but that's my highest offer off the bat."

"I'll take it." Loren jumped at the offer.

"Now, Loren, listen to me carefully."

Loren leaned in, as if Coco was about to instill some great secret. "Keep this money as cash. Hide it in your daughter's room, or somewhere your husband won't look. This way, if anything happens, you can grab it and go. I always believe that we women need to have a chunk of money hidden just in case we need to go off the grid for a little bit. You never know."

"Okay, I will."

"Don't you worry, honey. Just because he's the mayor don't mean his shit is all Shinola."

Adeline wrapped an arm around Loren and tugged her close. "Don't ask. Don't ask how she knows who you are, or who your husband is. The woman knows everything, it's scary. And for god's sake, don't ask about the whole shit and Shinola thing, she'll just tell you it's some Tonga saying."

Coco moved to the back of the store, reached into the coffee pot, and pulled out a stack of rolled bills before walking back to the group. "This is five thousand."

"Coco, when are you going to get a safe?" Melanie asked.

"When I can get one without some company having to install it. I don't want someone out there knowing that I have a safe, or where it is, or how to access it. Until then, I hide a little here and a little there. Besides, I can just call you girls and say the magic words."

"Please?" Sunday asked.

"Nah. Can we make this look like an accident?"

Loren's eyes were wide as she took in Coco's words and wondered whether the woman was serious.

But Coco was off on her next topic, her eyes sparked with excitement. Well, about as much of it as Coco ever really showed. "Olivia, look what I got in, a Smith & Wesson MP Shield. I don't think the thing has ever been fired." Coco pulled out the compact 9mm gun, along with an entire box of other items. "Took in several sets of brass knuckles. Tell me, who the hell still carries brass knuckles? Seems so *days of the rumble* to me. Nowadays, someone just caps your ass."

"What's this?" Loren held up a pink device that resembled a vegetable peeler.

"That's a stun gun. Just takes two triple-A batteries and will have a guy searching for his balls."

"Hmmm. I doubt that would really work. What's this?" Loren held up something that resembled a boxy-style toy gun.

"That's a Taser." Coco said it, then erupted in screams. "Fuck," Coco yelled as her knees went out from under her. The nearly six-foot-five woman, who was as wide as she was tall, hit the floor, boxes tumbling down around herg.

"Oh my god, I'm sorry. I'm sorry. I don't know what happened," Loren half-shouted, half-cried as she ran over and knelt next to Coco.

"Why don't you step back, Loren, I'm not sure we want you in Coco's reach?" Adeline wrapped one arm around her and pulled her back.

"Give me that." Olivia snatched the Taser from Loren's hands before she could accidentally hit the trigger again and send a second burst of energy pulsing through Coco.

"I'm so sorry, Coco." Tears bubbled in Loren's eyes.

"Out, get out. Just go." Coco pointed toward the door.

"I'm sorry, really."

"Go."

The girls chuckled as they stepped forward and each extended a hand to help Coco up. She ignored all of them. They knew what it felt like to be Tasered—hell, they each had to be Tasered when they were getting certified in their different weapons classes.

"Are you sure you're all right?" Adeline knelt next to the giant woman.

"Go before I break your scrawny neck."

Adeline looked up and saw the Taser that Olivia was waving to get her attention, and felt a bit relieved seeing that it was a twelve-hundred volt and not the standard fifty-thousand. Sure, it stung, but even static electricity was stronger. For Coco, it was all pride.

"Love you, Coco, talk soon," Adeline hollered as she headed for the back door and then stepped out.

Chapter Seven

RILEY

*R*iley couldn't believe he'd agreed to this, or that he trusted anything that came out of that woman's mouth. Maybe that was because he was too busy thinking of other things that he'd like to do to her mouth to worry about what kind of stunt she was pulling.

He felt his cock growing hard as he admired the firm ass of the woman leaning over the side of the car. She was looking at the engine and talking to Melanie, but he couldn't see what they were pointing at.

Adeline straightened, flicked her hair back, then turned to face him, a smile radiating across her face that sent his libido into overdrive.

"My, my look what the cat drug in, I truly didn't expect you to show."

"We made an agreement and I always keep my word."

"Mm-hmm. Well, don't worry, I'll take it easy on you. Sometimes I can be a little rough with the stick shift." Adeline licked her lips, and he could tell that she was thoroughly enjoying yanking his chain. Fine, two could play that game.

Like a python, he snapped one arm out and wrapped it around her waist, pulling her in. "Thank you, Adeline, but I like it rough"—he placed his mouth next to her ear—"and as far as stick shift . . . manual is for teenagers. I'm fully automatic and can go all night long." The heat from his breath radiated up Adeline's cheeks, and Riley mentally gave himself a high-five. He liked sexual barbs with a woman, but he was used to it being in the privacy of a bedroom, not out in the open where almost anyone could witness. "So, tell me, exactly what are you going to show me?" Riley kneaded his fingers against Adeline's hips.

Adeline pulled back and righted herself. "I'm going to teach you how to handle a real woman." She pointed over to a vintage Mustang. "All men need to know how to properly handle something with power. You can thank me later." She placed her fingers over his lips before he had a chance to say anything else.

One of the pit crewmen from Zotz came over and handed Riley a flame-retardant jumpsuit and a helmet.

"Just slide it on over your clothes," Adeline ordered before leaning forward and gathering her hair into a ponytail as she chanted, "helmet hair, I don't care."

"What did you say?"

"Nothing." Adeline ignored him. "Okay, I'll take you for a few laps first so you can get accustomed to the feel of speed and see how I operate, then we can switch seats and you take the wheel."

"I think that this is stupid, how often do you need tactical driving as a private investigator?"

"Great question, I'll show you. Because you see, not all husbands or mistresses want to be discovered, and not all husbands are willing to let their wives go so easily, especially not when careers or millions of dollars are on the line."

Melanie pulled back and then closed the hood before saying, "Checked battery cables, reset speedometer."

Riley arched a brow.

"What?" Adeline was peeved. "I'll teach anyone who wants to learn, but Melanie adjusts the speed so they think they are going faster than they truly are. It's a safety measure."

"Who *are* you guys?" Riley asked with a hint of sarcasm.

Adeline winked at him as she walked to the driver's side and hopped in through the window, since the doors were welded shut. "First things first, this is a five-point safety harness." Adeline slid her arms into the straps and then grabbed each side of the waist belts and clicked them in front of her. Finally she brought the fifth belt up from between her legs before connecting all of them together to make the five-point star.

Riley mimicked Adeline's steps.

Adeline fought back a giggle, started the engine, and then put the car in gear. Pedal to the metal, Adeline spun her wheels, the tail end fishtailing before grabbing traction and lurching forward.

"We have this set up as an obstacle course, so at different intervals"—Adeline grabbed hold of the wheel and swerved to the left, her tires squealing before she straightened her wheel and resumed to full speed—"objects will pop out in front of us, the idea is not to hit them."

Riley gripped the edge of his seat as Adeline yanked the steering wheel to the left then to the right. "I've had mistresses throw large garbage cans in front of me while I was driving."

She hit the brakes, and he jerked forward. She hit the gas, and he pressed back into the seat. "I've had angry men who were busted for boinking the nanny throw entire boxes of roofing nails out their window at me."

Catching a glimpse of the speedometer, Riley cringed as he saw the needle rising past eighty, ninety, one hundred. "How fast do you normally go?"

Swerve, brake, speed back up.

"Oh, I don't know." Adeline sounded as cool as shit as she spoke. "Maybe one-eighty or so."

"Great, just great." Riley felt the sweat prickle along his forehead and slice down his back.

Swerve, brake, speed back up.

"Last stretch, ready for your turn?" Adeline shouted with glee as she sped up even faster, heading right for the wall.

Riley's heart raced, holy fuck, the bitch was going to kill them. They were going to die. "Brakes. Brakes."

"Oh yeah, knew that I forgot something." Adeline threw her foot down and pulled her emergency brake, tires spinning, the smell of burning rubber filling the car as it rotated once, twice, and then came to a complete stop almost exactly where they'd begun.

Riley couldn't get out of the fucking harness fast enough. Unclipping the damn things, he ripped them off, then jumped out of the window and staggered from the Mustang, looking half-dazed.

The workers of Zotz raced over with first-aid kit and water bottles. Although the car was fine and Riley appeared fine, the Iron Ladies and Zotz took every precaution. They still had the track medic check the blood pressure and eye pupils of all drivers after their "Adeline experience" as Zotz liked to call it. As they examined him, he listened to her talk with the other ladies.

"How did I do?"

"Holy shit, Adeline, I think that was your best stop ever, look"—Melanie pointed to the front tires of the car—"I think you're within five inches of your starting point. Good job."

Riley shook his head, the woman was crazy, but she could fucking drive. He had to give her that.

When Riley was given the all clear, Adeline tossed him the keys. "Your turn."

He laughed as he scanned up and down Adeline's body. "I'll leave it to you. You definitely know how to handle a stick shift."

Something fired in Adeline's eyes, and he could tell she was dying to say something but was obviously happy with this small victory instead.

They each took a bottle of water that was offered to them by Melanie, and Riley found himself concentrating a bit too hard on the way Adeline wrapped her mouth around the top of the bottle, and the way her neck moved as she swallowed the cool liquid.

"So Mr. Thomas, exactly what is it that you do?"

"Besides give you a hard time?"

"Oh that was hard?"

Riley choked as his water went down the wrong pipe. "Sweetheart, I haven't even shown you hard yet but I will. And once I do, I promise you won't be left questioning."

Adeline was left dumbfounded, her mouth open a bit in awe. That look on her face, Riley loved and all he could think was, what he wouldn't give to have her lips wrapped around something else.

"So, what is it you do to earn money because I know that giving me a hard time isn't it?" Adeline punched Riley's shoulder, snapping him from his thoughts and the one-way track his mind was headed down.

"I'm sorry, what did you ask?"

"What do you do? You know, as in work. The daily grind?" Adeline rolled her eyes at him and Riley fought back the urge to lean in and kiss her when she least expected it.

"I own RT Land, it's a development company. In a

nutshell, I purchase property and then use it for larger projects. If there is an area in need of a shopping plaza, medical offices, or even homes, then I front the money and build it on my property. When it is close to complete, I start looking for buyers."

"Impressive."

Riley didn't tell her that up until now it wasn't all that impressive, but after spending just this short time with Adeline he was seriously thinking, how could he use his land to help others and still have a successful career?

Chapter Eight

LOREN

*L*oren raced around the house; she needed to get her head clear before Greg got home. At least fifty times today she'd questioned whether the Iron Ladies had given her the right advice in pawning Greg's golf clubs.

After settling Noelle into bed for the night, Loren made her way out to the living room and was sitting on the couch reading a book when she heard the garage door open. She pressed the home button on her phone and then turned on audio recording. Sliding the phone next to her so that it was hidden by the chair cushions, she glanced at the clock on the fireplace mantle and sighed. Just a little bit more and this would all be over, she told herself.

Bracing herself for whatever mood Greg was in when he walked in, she took several deep breaths as he opened the door and stepped in. "Hi, Greg, there's a plate for you in the microwave just press reheat. You're running late."

"Yep, was a crazy day so I went and hit a game of golf with a couple of the guys. I got a par three on a par-five hole."

"Wow, that's incredible, is that because of your golf clubs?"

"You have no clue what a par three on a par five is, do you Loren? I'm actually very good at golf, which is why I bought those clubs in the first place. They didn't make me a great player, they only improved my game. I probably could have gone pro if I'd wanted to."

"Oh sorry, I didn't know. So those clubs are working out for you."

"Yes, they're working out, in fact several of the guys were just admiring them today."

"That's nice dear."

If Greg had been paying attention to anyone but himself, he would have noticed the slight shake in Loren's voice. She wasn't hurt, no, those days were gone...she was pissed. He'd stood there and told her a boldface lie. She knew all too well that there was no way he played golf today, or if he did, it wasn't with his golf clubs. And no one admired them, since patrons at Queen's Gold were now admiring them.

She felt like an idiot for questioning the ladies; they'd been right. She inwardly smiled, this was just like the milk-shake when she was a teenager...totally vindicated.

"I think I have what all I need. I need to go over to the courthouse and see if I can discover anything about Loren's property, it's really bugging me. If he has gotten his hands on it, I want to know how, and I want every single name involved in the transaction. Plus, I want to try to talk with a few of these interns and set a pattern for Greg's temperament." Adeline snagged her purse from under her desk and then stacked her papers, but stopped when the elevator dinged and off walked, or rather, bounced, Melanie.

"You must be having a great morning."

"Oh, I am, and the rest of you are about to as well." Melanie's eyes were beaming with excitement as she pulled a manila envelope out of her bag for each of them.

"Someone's been busy," Adeline teased.

Everyone opened their envelopes and unfolded the stacks of papers they found inside.

"Highlighted blueprints?" Olivia glanced up just long enough to shoot Melanie a curious look.

"Happy Help employee badges?" Adeline examined the lanyard and tag. "What, we're maids now?"

"An itinerary? Ohhh, minute by minute." Sunday was the only one impressed.

"I also have uniforms for all of you. I called in one of our favors. I promised her that we'd be in and out and wouldn't bother with any office other than Greg's."

"When are we doing this?" Adeline looked less than excited.

"Tonight. The cleaning crew goes in at nine and is out by ten. We are responsible for cleaning that one office. There are security guards, so make sure to have your badge on in case they swing though. We have one main key between the four of us, so we'll stay together. If he's hiding anything, we will find it."

"Oh, what a beautiful morning, oh, what a beautiful day. What I wouldn't give to see the wake-up call coming his way," Adeline sang.

"You really can be a bitch, Adeline, you know that?"

Adeline nodded at Sunday's question, not at all offended.

"Oh, and just in case you're interested . . ." Sunday clicked on another screen and then read. "Riley Thomas, age thirty-four. Never married. Land developer, owner of RT Land, owns a condo in Vista Cay, which he paid cash for. Except for two years at the community college, I couldn't find any other schooling. He is considered a self-made millionaire and has spent the last ten years building his company. Background checks came back clean. It appears that he's solid."

"Not interested." Adeline winked at Sunday.

"Sure you aren't. The sparks are electric between you two."

"You want to know what's electric? The chair. The one I want to strap his ass to."

"Good god, would you like me to pass him a note in study hall?" Olivia rolled her eyes. "Let's get our asses to work. I'm dying to shoot something or break something." Olivia stood and everyone groaned at her tough-as-nails comment.

～

At eight thirty, the four women stood in the back of the Iron Ladies office building near a side room that they kept locked at all times. It would open for any one of the four ladies only. If anyone else tried, they wouldn'tt be able to break into operation control, and all they'd get would be lots of alarms. This was their secret headquarters, where all things were kept. This was the one room that let people know they weren't dealing with just ordinary businesswomen or everyday dicks, which was why no one but the four ladies entered this room.

Adeline placed her hand on the panel, let the scanner do its thing, and grinned when the door clicked. It really was music to her ears. They each grabbed a pair of rubber-soled shoes and thin leather gloves and quickly changed into the uniforms Melanie had provided before snagging their utility belts and confirming that all of the necessary equipment was attached. They ran through everything required for what they liked to call their best behavior: breaking, entering, searching, and data-transfer operations.

"I've got new proxies for our IP address set." Sunday flipped open a small laptop. "I'm already logged into the city's computer security system. I'll be able to reroute the camera's pan and tilt function so that it isn't sweeping across you."

"Cameras, mics, and earpieces on." Adeline gave a thumbs-up and looked to Melanie, Olivia, and Sunday as she waited for each of them to give the signal.

After strapping on her gun under her maid's uniform, she added a few extra rounds of ammunition in her pockets, just in case. A small bottle of mace and a stun gun that doubled as a flashlight made their way into her purse as well.

They locked up their central command and headed out of their office and to the Porsche Cayenne they used for these kinds of operations. They liked it for speed, but they liked it more because it was black and had the maximum five-percent window tinting allowed. The automated license plate cover that would slide down at the click of a button was an added bonus.

Orlando City Hall was just a few miles away, but it was set back from the road.

"Do you remember when the old city hall blew up?" Adeline was the oldest of the four by almost five years, and the memory of her dad holding her and watching the fire still thrilled her.

"Umm no. When was this?"

"Ninety-one, I think. Warner Brothers studio paid for the explosion."

"What the fuck? Why have I never heard this?" Olivia was seated in the front passenger seat while Adeline drove. They all faced her, not wanting to miss a single word.

"It was huge, Mel Gibson and Danny Glover were here, and it was used for the opening of *Lethal Weapon* three. When the two of them were arguing over the red or blue wire and then they realized that they cut the wrong one, so he says, "*Grab the cat,*" and they run out as it explodes."

"Holy shit, I never knew that. We are so going to have to rewatch that movie."

"Sounds good to me." Adeline could use some good girl-bonding time.

At nine o'clock on the dot the ladies parked by City Hall, and Sunday scanned the perimeter once more via the small laptop before switching to the screen to her iPad mini. "Okay, let's go," Sunday gave the order. "Just act normal."

Melanie opened the back hatch of their vehicle and handed a plastic basket full of cleaning supplies to Olivia, the vacuum went to Adeline, and the stack of dusters went to Sunday. Melanie propped her own basket of supplies on her hip before she closed the trunk.

A guard was standing at the door, and he barely looked up from his phone long enough to glance at their badges and open the door for them. On the fourth floor, Melanie pulled out the key and unlocked the outer door to Greg's office, then the four of them quickly moved to the far office on the left. The plaque on the door read: Mayor Greg Delaney. Again, Melanie opened the door and they filed in. What would probably look like a rehearsed dance to an outsider was just good training to the ladies. They set their equipment down, slid on their gloves, and split to opposite ends of the room. Adeline moved to each set of windows and closed the blinds. Sunday pulled out her small laptop from inside her uniform and grabbed several memory sticks. Olivia placed an amplifier that fed into their earpieces at the base of the door so they would hear anyone coming long before they got to the door. Melanie pulled out her lock-picking tools and set about moving from cabinet to drawer, unlocking each one.

Olivia was right there, opening the drawers, pulling files, and snapping pictures of the contents. When Olivia moved to the next cabinet, Adeline stepped in and slid her gloved hands to the back of each drawer and cabinet, feeling for hidden compartments or loose edges. Right then it was all about speed, divide and conquer was their motto.

"Bingo." Adeline felt like she'd just hit the jackpot.

"What is it?" Olivia asked, but didn't stop snapping photos of files.

"This drawer has a false back." Adeline lifted it from the rollers, pressing the locks that held the sliding rail into place, and then set the whole thing on the ground. After pulling her utility knife off her belt, she flipped to her awl tool and slid the pointed tip into the crevice and then dragged it along the seam. The faux-backing gave a satisfying pop that was almost orgasmic to Adeline. Inside lay a stack of papers. Adeline pulled them out and flipped through them, quickly spreading them out and then looking over to get Olivia's attention, but she was already there, capturing images of each one.

Sunday kept the cameras panning away from the office areas via her laptop and kept downloading information from Greg's computer while the other three searched.

"Let's go." Olivia shoved the stack of files back into Adeline's hands. "Alphabetical order." Adeline nodded, making quick work of setting everything back to right. Then Melanie began locking the cabinets and drawers.

"Stop." Sunday held up her hand. "Fuck. Greg's here. Hide." Grabbing the box of cleaning supplies and vacuum, Olivia darted for the door, snagging the amplifier on her way. Sunday closed her laptop, gathered the memory sticks, and picked up the rest of the unused cleaning supplies, hoping to god they'd be forgiven for not getting the office cleaned, and darted out to the main area. Adeline and Melanie finished shoving all the papers back into their correct positions and locking the cabinets.

Adeline jumped when Greg's door opened once more, but it was Sunday and Olivia standing there.

"Hurry, I think he just got onto the elevator." Olivia looked behind her.

"Where are the cleaning supplies? Melanie looked around.

"We stashed them out in the main office area."

Adeline had just closed the last file and put it back into the proper position when they all froze. The sound of voices echoed around them.

"Shit, there's no time. Come on." Adeline moved to a large bank of cabinets that sat in a row under Greg's window.

Pulling the door open, she let out a small laugh. "Perfect. Get in."

"What the fuck?" Melanie was adamantly shaking her head but stopped as the voices grew closer and their places to hide seemed to have been narrowed down to exactly where Adeline had directed.

Olivia, Sunday, and Melanie dove for cabinet doors, each folding their bodies up and crawling inside.

"God, let's just hope he doesn't keep condoms in one of these," Melanie muttered.

"Oh, he doesn't. He keeps those in his center desk drawer, I saw them." Adeline replied.

"Will you two shut up?" Sunday snapped, freaked that they were going to get caught.

"Turn your recorder on Sunday." Adeline instructed.

"I will—" Her words cut off when the office door opened.

Adeline couldn't miss the telltale sound of the door locking, or the high-pitch laugh of a woman who most definitely wasn't Loren.

"That's not Mrs. Chatham," she whispered, craning her neck as far as she could when no one answered.

Olivia had her small camera up against the crack trying to snap photos, and Melanie and Sunday were both glaring at Adeline for making noise.

Melanie lifted a silent hand and then pointed to the amplifier that was tucked by Olivia's feet.

Sunday turned the receiver toward the cabinet door, and Greg and his female companion's voices came through their earpieces.

Adeline was all for watching some porn, but Greg Delaney getting it on while still wearing his shoes and socks was a hard no. Listening to the girl gag as she tried to give him a blowjob had Adeline fighting her every instinct to shout, *just fucking breathe through your nose.*

His attempt at dirty talk? It was terrible. She was now convinced that helping Loren was more of a mission than an assignment. No woman should be subjected to a lover like that.

Adeline was stiff, she ached, she had no clue how long they'd been crammed into these cabinets and the two of them were still going at it. She moved and her knee popped. Melanie, Olivia, and Sunday jerked their heads and stared at her.

"*What?*" she mouthed. She always hated it that when she was trying to be quiet, everything she did seemed ten times louder. Like when she was younger and was just starting her rebellious phase, it always seemed that the stairs in your house were suddenly louder than the fucking philharmonic orchestra. She let out a small laugh. Or street lights that you'd never really noticed prior to that night were suddenly shining at five-thousand lumens each. At that thought, Adeline quickly looked around to make sure that no lights could shine into the cabinets.

Adeline blinked and tried to keep the sweat from rolling into her eyes as she crouched and then it hit her: she had to pee. No, she didn't just have to pee, she had to *pee*, like she was turning yellow she had to pee so bad, and she couldn't understand why, because just a few seconds ago, it wasn't bothering her. She blamed the, venti, half-sweet, non-fat caramel macchiato with an extra shot and whipped cream from Starbucks she drank before they embarked on this shit show.

"Yes, yes, oh, god, oh god."

The woman's fake moans were enough to distract Adeline, who had to clamp her hand over her lips to keep from laughing.

Thank god—not Greg, Adeline only had to sit there about ten minutes more until Greg and his latest tart left the office.

Sunday gave the all clear, and the four of them crawled out, all of them unable to stand just yet because they had so many aches.

Adeline ran and used Greg's en-suite bathroom.

Walking out of the office, they gathered their cleaning supplies, Sunday logged into their security system and disarmed the alarms that had been reset since it way past ten, and they waited for the all-clear before exiting.

"Give the man credit, he has stamina." Olivia chuckled.

They drove the six miles home.

Chapter Ten

ADELINE

"*H*ello?" Adeline answered the office line.

"Hey, it's me, who all is there?"

"Everyone. Want me to put you on speaker?"

"Please."

Adeline placed her hand over the receiver and shouted for Sunday and Melanie to come over. "Olivia is on the phone." When they'd all pulled up a seat, Adeline pressed speaker. "We're all here, Livi."

"Sunday, I just uploaded several hundred photos. You all can take a look, but I hate to say this, I can't find anything."

"Except for him sneaking away with Mrs. Chatham," Melanie replied.

"Well, yeah, except for that. I just don't see him doing anything else. Are we sure we aren't on some wild goose chase, and that Loren isn't just hoping we'll find something so she can get even more?"

The frustration was bleeding in every word. Olivia had been monitoring Greg Delaney's every movement and activity for the last few weeks and hadn't turned up anything they could use.

"He goes to City Hall every morning and stays there all day. I've followed him to several lunches, and he actually went on lunches. His affairs are carried on after work hours. I hate to say it, but I can't find anything else shady. I went through all of the photos from last night and moved anything that was clearly not pertinent to a file, but if it might be the least bit interesting I've forwarded it, I also sent photos from the few lunches that I caught on camera. Let me know if you see something that I didn't."

"Thanks, Livi."

"I'll be at the office in a bit. I need to take a nap, I was up all night going through those."

"Take it easy, we've got this." Adeline pressed disconnect then scooted her chair around to face to the large television screen.

Melanie had grabbed the remote control and turned it on, and Sunday sent the first file to the screen.

"Can you lay the photos out in a tile format, so we can see several at the same time? I want to compare them. We have to be missing something." Adeline had one main philosophy, and that was Occam's razor: the simplest solution was usually the correct one. So, she looked for the simplest answer within the pictures.

"Okay, what do we see?" She leaned in and looked at each.

"His personal secretary is a guy. So, to the public, it appears that his only close connection to a woman is his wife and the few interns who work in the office."

"That's how he has avoided gossip." Melanie leaned forward as she spoke and focused on the photos.

"According to the date on that photo it was taken on a Saturday. It is summer in Orlando. Seems to me that he either is always wearing a suit, or is working hard to maintain his appearance. He doesn't want anyone to see him relax."

"Look at this photo." Adeline pointed. "I think that is Capital Grille, and this one"—she pointed to another—"is Capital Grille. All of his meetings are in upscale places, places where his highest contributors would dine. Is he doing that to make a connection so they see him as an equal, or so they see him having legitimate meetings in public places?"

"Or so the taxpayers are paying for those hundred-to-two-hundred-dollar meals?" Melanie asked, her tone full of disdain.

"Okay, so he seems perfect from the outside. Chivalrous, charming, pleasant, would you both agree?" Adeline looked at Sunday and Melanie for their agreement.

Sunday clicked and brought up the next set of tiled pictures. "These seem pretty innocent, Greg reading newspapers. Greg and his secretary at a fundraiser."

"I'm sorry, but I always hated the fakeness of politicians and the baby-kissing bullshit. Look at him, he's sweating like a whore in church, but he gets out of his car to walk the streets just to turn heads and attract attention. And really . . . who the hell wants a selfie with him? Look at him holding that damn selfie stick, did he come with his own?"

Sunday took a screenshot of the photo then minimized the screen. She opened another page and uploaded the photo, and they all waited as TinEye searched the billions of online photos. "The photo was posted on Instagram. 'Man of the People' is the tagline. 'Mayor Delaney spends the day with the people of Orlando. He's never too busy for a selfie.' It looks like the image was uploaded by Greg himself."

Sunday scrolled through to another set of photos and clicked tile format. "These all look boring . . . coffee, newspaper, what appears to be a district meeting, dinner with Loren and the Chathams?"

"How quaint," Melanie scoffed. "Next."

Adeline held a hand up. "Wait, zoom in on the picture with the Chathams."

When it was filling the screen, Adeline grinned. "Do you see that...is that her purse? It isn't a briefcase, look . . . his briefcase is on the other side of him."

Sunday zoomed in on the spot Adeline was pointing to.

"Looks to me like he's dropping a note into her purse," Melanie said, none too impressed.

"That isn't a note, that's some kind of document. It's folded, but look right there"—Adeline stood and walked over to the screen and pointed—"those are typed letters, you can barely see them through the paper, but they are typed."

"Maybe it's about their next liaison, or maybe it's just a piece of paper about the fucking Junior League?"

Adeline shook her head at Melanie's statement. "Not buying it."

"There isn't anything in the photo that indicates something shady."

"Sunday, can you find the photos of the forms I found in the hidden compartment?"

Sunday rapidly flipped through pictures and then brought them up, they were photos of a land deed under the name LeAen Holdings and a bill of sale to Tertiary Development.

"Why would he hide these? Sunday, see what you can find out about either of these companies."

"Will do."

"Up until now, we've only seen what Greg wants us to see. We need to get closer. Olivia can't keep tailing him, and let's be honest, everything he's doing seems up front to the naked eye. Until we find out what he has going on with these companies that he needs to keep secretive, I'm not sure where we go next." Melanie leaned back in her chair and folded her hands behind her head.

"What exactly are you suggesting?" Sunday asked.

"We get up close and personal. We need to become friends with him, get into his inner circle. He isn't home enough for us to do the housekeeper or nanny act. Sunday, can you look to see if there are any positions open at City Hall?"

"On it." Sunday nodded and started searching online.

"Let's see if Loren can host a dinner party." Melanie was still coming up with ideas.

"I'd say play golf, but obviously, he is only interested in sinking a different kind of ball," Adeline said as she fought to hold back her laugh.

"Really?" Melanie shook her head. "What about Riley?"

"What about him?"

"We could use Riley to get to the mayor." Melanie arched a brow. "Didn't Sunday mention a land deal? Riley is a land developer? Maybe that's the in we need. That guy will do anything to help his sister." Melanie exaggerated a wink. "You could pretend to be his girlfriend."

"I don't want to pretend."

"I know that you don't."

"That isn't what I meant, Melanie, and you know it."

"I know no such thing." Melanie stared at her thought-fully. "Seriously, though, I think this is it, truly. Think about it. Riley owns a company that does land development. We think that Greg is doing something shady with Loren's property. Playing off those two things could get us close enough to figure out what the hell is going on."

Adeline glared, knowing that Melanie was right. That this was the way in. But how could she turn this so she didn't come across as inept by asking for his help? The man would rather chew glass than do anything for her. She racked her brain and no ideas flashed before her, so she bid her goodbye and went to where she did her best thinking . . . Neiman Marcus.

After a few hours of retail therapy Adeline headed home, it was just after ten at night. Exhausted, she tossed the bags onto her bed, pulled out her cell phone, and dialed Riley. A little piece of her hoped that the call would go straight to voicemail.

"Hello?" His voice was deep, and Adeline shivered.

"Mr. Thomas, this is Adeline Morgan with the Iron Ladies, I'm sorry to be calling you so late."

"Hey, Adeline, that's okay. Is something wrong? Is Loren all right?"

Why did the man have to be so damn nice, why now? His first questions were to make sure that nothing was wrong and his sister was okay? God, he was a regular Casa-fuckin-nova. "Yes, everything is fine. I . . .I mean, we were wondering if you'd be willing to come in and talk with us at your earliest convenience?"

"Can I ask what about?"

"We have an idea that might help you get your rezoning and help your sister at the same time." Adeline was pleased by this ingenious little breakthrough.

"Okay, I can come in tomorrow. I have a meeting at nine, but after that, I can head to you. It might be close to eleven, if that's okay."

"That's fine."

"Oh and Adeline?"

"Yes?"

"Something that you should know about me, I would do anything for the women in my life."

"Well, Loren is a lucky girl to have a brother like you then. Thank you. I . . . we look forward to seeing you." Damn it all to hell, she'd almost said I again, as if she was the one who wanted to see him. She sooo didn't, he got on her nerves, all seven trillion of them. Besides that, he was an ass, an ass with a gorgeous body, good job, and huge heart. *I'd do anything for the women in my life*. What the fuck was that supposed to mean, why didn't he just say his sister? And was this really for his sister, or for her? God, she had no clue anymore.

Chapter Eleven

ADELINE

*A*deline sat in the parking lot at the courthouse and felt a little like Inspector Gadget as she slid her gun from its holster and into her glove box. Before closing it, she grabbed her purse and pulled out her handcuffs, her stun gun, and her mace. Shaking her handbag so everything jostled a bit, she looked once more just to make sure she wasn't forgetting anything. She was about to go through metal detectors and the courthouse officers wouldn't take too kindly to her bringing in a weapon. Once she was sure she wouldn't be arrested, she locked her glove box and climbed out of her car.

As she walked in, Adeline waved to several deputies and cops that she knew. Even though the Iron Ladies were private investigators, they worked very closely with their local law enforcement, since it made their job so much easier.

Once through security, she took the elevator up to the tax office and then waited in line for Belle.

"Hello, Adeline, what brings you here today?"

"Hey, I need to see if you can look up two properties for me."

"What's the address of the first one?"

"Ninety-four-oh-five Snow Queen Drive."

Belle typed and waited. "What information do you need?"

"The owner."

"Looks like it is owned by Tertiary Development, the signer on the closing forms was Trinity Reynolds."

Adeline wrote the information down, wondering how this Trinity played into the whole Hillary/Greg affair. "Okay, the second property is undeveloped. I have the assessor process number."

She rattled off the numbers, and after Belle had it pulled up, her expression turned confused.

"The property was owned by Loren Delaney, but a quit claim deed was filed about fourteen months ago. There is currently no name on record, which is bizarre."

"Believe it or not, we've found several weird things lately."

"I'll look into this a bit more and pull the official copy of the deed."

"Thanks, Belle." Adeline turned, and as she walked back to her car, she sent the information that she'd just learned in a group text to the rest of the Iron Ladies.

The next item on her list of things to do was to call Barrett, their favorite attorney, a partner at Morgan and Stern. She needed information on Deena Charles, who just happened to be a PA at his firm.

"Yo."

"Hey, Adeline, what's up?"

"How closely do you work with Deena Charles?"

"Oh god." His groan was mixed with a chuckle. "Pretty close, she's my filer."

"Perfect. Got a few minutes for me? I'm just across the street at the court house."

"Sure."

They hung up, Adeline drove the block and a half over to

Barrett's law firm's parking lot. When she got out, he was waiting for her.

"So what exactly do you need?"

Adeline looked Barrett up and down and, not for the first time, wished that she felt something for him. The man was gorgeous, but every time Adeline saw him, she saw a brother. "I need to get her to tell me about Greg Delaney's temper and why she left her internship at the mayor's office after only six months."

"How do you propose to get her talk to you?"

Adeline smiled. "Sisterhood." She kissed her fist and thumped her chest.

But Adeline quickly discovered that not all women were as committed to sisterhood as she was.

"Anything, something that can point me in the right direction." She hated lying, but sometimes it was a necessary evil. "My client is young and scared. She thinks that she is all alone. Can you tell me about his temper, did he make any inappropriate advances, anything?"

"I'm sorry, Ms. Morgan, but I just don't remember."

Adeline wanted to smack the woman, it had only been three years ago, she hadn't fucking forgotten anything. "Can I leave you my number in case your memory suddenly comes back? Hopefully you remember something soon, I'm really worried for her and would hate for anything to happen, especially if it was something that could be avoided." When lying didn't work, guilt sometimes did the trick.

"Anything I say is off the record?"

"Absolutely. It's considered hearsay until you give a statement."

Deena fiddled with her hands for several seconds before casting a nervous glance around the room and whispering, "I married my high school sweetheart right after graduation."

"So you were married during your time as an intern?"

Deena nodded.

"Did this cause a problem?"

"He made me uncomfortable. He never did anything that could be taken as inappropriate, but he definitely made plenty of opportunities available."

"What do you mean?"

"He always asked me to accompany him to meetings, and then he'd insist that I ride with him, so it was just the two of us in the car. He'd have me doing stuff in his office with the door closed, and even staying late. He never made a move, but he did give me plenty of opportunities to make one if I was interested. He even made several comments about his wife not understanding him and being overworked and needing to relax. I don't know, I was just uncomfortable, which is why I've never said anything. What if I was just reading something into it and he wasn't freaky like that? I don't want to be responsible for ruining someone's career or marriage just because I read the situation wrong, so I left."

"What about his temper?"

"What temper? I never saw him lose his temper, he was always methodically reserved."

"Methodically reserved, that's an astute observation. Thanks, Deena, for your time. Still take my number just in case you remember anything else." Adeline handed over the card that held only her name and cell number.

On her way out, she stopped to say goodbye to Barrett and then headed back to the Iron Ladies office. She had about twenty minutes before Riley was due.

She had just gotten comfy and seated behind her desk, and was feeling decidedly less assured about the plan they had hatched last night. The plan they had hatched? No, it was more like, the plan Melanie had concocted. Because for all of Adeline's outward bravado, the reality was it only served as a useful mask to hide her deep-seated inner insecurities. She'd hidden it from almost everyone and managed to keep up the tough-girl act over these past few years. Yet, it seemed like the first time in god knew how long that there was a guy Adeline found attractive, and he wasn't falling at her feet. No, he seemed to despise her . . . damn it all . . . not to mention that he was related to a client.

And she was going to have to use him as part of the decoy and spend a large amount of time with him. Damn, damn, triple damn. She gave herself a mental shake, the heels, lipstick, and diva attitude might not be the real Adeline, but it was all that she was willing to let anyone see, no one needed to know that she was really emotional and often felt like a vulnerable piece of crap.

Adeline was scanning social media posts of the other interns and cringed every time she read another comment about Greg Delaney and his assumed perfection. "Perfect, my ass. More like perfect douche." She continued compiling a list of the mayor's body language, who he seemed to lean closer to, and where his eyes appeared to be looking in each photo.

"Holy shit, holy shit, I've got it. You aren't going to believe this." Sunday knocked over her chair as she jumped up from her computer. All three women snapped their heads up and waited for Sunday to calm down enough to speak. "I got it. LeAen, Tertiary, and Greg Dela—"

The elevator doors opened, stopping Sunday mid-sentence, and out walked Riley.

"Fuck," they all said in unison.

"Wow, I can't remember the last time I received such a warm welcome."

Adeline hurried over to welcome him. "Sorry, it wasn't directed at you, truthfully."

"Sure it wasn't." Riley sounded somewhat comforted by Adeline's words, and she was relieved to hear him joking.

"No, I'm serious. Sunday was just getting ready to tell us

something exciting, and we were all waiting to hear it when the elevator dinged and scared us, that's all."

"Don't let me stop you, continue. I can wait until you all are done." He didn't take his eyes off Adeline as he said that, and for some reason, Adeline felt that there was a hidden meaning in those words.

She turned to meet three sets of eyes, but as usual, it was Melanie who spoke. "Why don't we get Riley caught up, and then Sunday can tell us all that is appropriate?"

Sunday nodded, and Adeline escorted Riley back to the boardroom, the others following. "Before we get started, would you like something to drink?" Adeline offered as she moved to the small, apartment-size fridge and grabbed a few bottles of water.

"Water is great."

She grabbed one for everyone and handed them out before taking her seat diagonal from Riley. "First, let me thank you for coming."

"It's not a problem, what can I do for you guys?"

"Well, what we are about to ask is out of the norm, but we are having trouble digging up information on a particular project that Greg is involved with. What I'm going to tell you needs to remain confidential, and we would like to keep Loren out of the loop until we have more information."

"I'm not okay with that." Riley set his bottle down, ready to call this meeting over.

"Riley, right now Loren is still vulnerable, if she learns too much too quickly without the proof to back it up, it will do one of two things: break her completely and she won't leave him because she'll feel worthless, or it will make her so angry that she will jeopardize our job and blow the entire operation. So . . . as you can probably guess, we aren't looking to withhold information just for the hell of it. We do it because neither of those options is one we want to navigate."

Clearly, Riley didn't like either option, but after a long moment, he sighed and leaned back in his seat. "What do you need from me?"

Adeline locked eyes with Melanie then Olivia and then Sunday, each giving her a nod. It was their silent permission to reveal their information and tactics. "Greg is having an affair. He meets with a woman, gets into her car, and they go off together." Adeline turned to Sunday, who was busy typing while Melanie got up and moved to turn on the television they had in the boardroom and turned it on. Seconds later, the photo of Greg and Hillary Chatham appeared on the screen.

Riley cringed.

Sunday typed and the next photo from the restaurant appeared.

"My sister knows her? Who is the other guy?"

"That's her husband, Councilman Chatham," Adeline answered.

"Fuck." Riley let out a long, exaggerated sigh, but Sunday continued clicking, and the photo zoomed in. "What's Greg doing?"

"He's putting a document of some sort into her purse, which is what has us curious. We've been looking into a few things, one of which is your sister's property that your grandparents left her. We found some documents that suggest that Greg might be using the property in some kind of land deal with the city, but that's just speculation right now."

"Do I want to know how you got the documents?"

"Nope." Adeline gave him a wink. "Anyway, we were just getting ready to find out more about our discovery when you walked in. Sunday . . ."

"Adeline found out that a quit claim was filed on the property a little over a year ago, but there isn't a name for the current owner. I have been searching ever since. Anyway, I finally found out that it was owned by a company called LeAen Holdings and the quit claim was with Tertiary Development."

"What the fuck?" Riley jumped from his seat.

"Hold on, Riley, let me finish." Sunday held up one hand. "Greg has been working with Tertiary Development on the land deal."

"Who owns LeAen Holdings?" Adeline looked puzzled.

"That was my grandparents' company. They turned every penny they ever made into property, a lot of it. When they passed, the land went into a trust for Loren and me. My mom was their only child, her name was LeAnne, so they took the last syllables from Riley and Loren and mom's name to come up with the name for the trust. But I'm not sure what Greg has to do with it, or how he could do a quit claim on it."

"By forging Loren's signature and getting a notary to falsify seeing her sign the documents."

Riley's face was slowly turning red as anger began to boil inside him.

"According to the documents we found, Tertiary is buying the property at just under forty dollars per acre—"

"No fucking way, the property is worth twenty times that, it is prime. The airport has offered to buy it for three million, but Loren wants to save it for Noelle, she actually had it set up into a trust under Noelle's name so that if anything ever did happen between her and Greg it didn't become part of a divorce settlement."

"And once we get all the proof, we will be able to get the property back for her, but until then, we need to stay calm. Let me continue. The other company, Tertiary . . . you've never heard of them because . . ." Sunday once again tapped on her keyboard and a series of photographs popped up on the screen. One was a yearbook photo.

"That's Greg," Riley added.

"Yep," Sunday agreed. "And the woman next to him is . . . are you ready for it? Hillary Trinity Reynolds."

"Hillary?" Olivia and Melanie asked in unison.

"Trinity?" Adeline asked, and they all smiled, because leave it to Adeline to pick up on the insignificant thing.

"Yep, it seems that Hillary Trinity and Hillary Chatham are one and the same. When she got married, she took her maiden name as her middle name, which I guess is a thing. It also makes sense that the company that owns her house is Tertiary Development."

"How exactly does that make sense?" Olivia asked.

"What does trinity mean?"

"The Father, Son, and Holy Ghost?"

Sunday shot Olivia an exasperated look and corrected her. "No, it *means* three. What else means three? Tertiary."

"But that could be a coincidence, right?" Riley didn't look at all convinced.

"It could be, if it weren't for the other thing I just found."

Melanie was all but vibrating in her seat as we waited for Sunday to lay it all out for us.

"Good god woman, can you tell us already and stop dragging it on?"

Sunday waved off her outburst. "Hold your horses Mel, I'm getting there. I just want to get the proof up on my screen so that I can show all of you. It took some digging, but I eventually found out that Tertiary Development was started by two students at Stetson University as part of their senior thesis. You following me?"

Everyone, including Riley, nodded.

"Those two students were..." Sunday pulled a photo up. "Greg and Hillary."

"Well, shit."

"Exactly," Sunday answered.

"So, Greg sold Loren's property to the company for pennies on the dollar and now the company is selling it to the city for fair market value? Why? Is he hiding the money from Loren and planning on leaving her?" Riley was dumbfounded over this revelation.

"We don't know yet, but we do know the city has made a bid to buy the property from Tertiary, believing that they are the rightful owner, for eight hundred and seventy-five dollars per acre, or just over four million dollars."

"So, I dug into Hillary a little more and found out that the house that she and Greg were going to was owned by—"

"Tertiary Development," Adeline answered, since she had already learned that from Belle.

Sunday smiled brightly, clearly loving when things fell into place.

"First, do Greg and Hillary still own Tertiary?" Adeline asked.

"Yes," Sunday answered.

Adeline jotted a note down in her notebook before looking up and adding in her two cents. "Then we need to find out what Greg's plans are for the money from Loren's property. Problem is, he doesn't want Loren to know that the property has been sold, nor where he's stashing the money. He was planning on keeping the money from his own fucking daughter."

"Motherfucker," Melanie hissed.

"Douchebag," Olivia groaned out.

"Typical male scum." Adeline wasn't that surprised. Sure, men were fun for a little bit, but they always ended up showing their true colors.

Riley didn't say anything about the derogatory comments on his own gender. "So what's the plan? How can we help my sister, save my niece's inheritance, and screw the motherfucking, douchebag, typical-male scum?"

All four ladies took in Riley's question, then realized how he took their words and let out a laugh. He returned Adeline's wink and damn it, she blushed.

"Okay, here's the plan." Adeline leaned forward and opened her notebook.

Chapter Twelve

RILEY

*R*iley sat in the lobby of the mayor's office. He was shocked that Greg had been able to make time for him on such short notice. But, as he sat there staring down at his watch, he was quickly wondering if Greg was playing some game, it was almost an hour past his appointment time. Riley shifted in the uncomfortable plastic chair and stared at the large portrait of Greg that hung on the wall.

Riley tapped his fingers on the arm of the chair as he checked the time again. He had no idea how this whole plan was going to work, after all, he and Adeline were going to be working closely, she was going to be pretending to be his girlfriend, which was clearly something she found distasteful.

So exactly why was he doing this again? Oh yeah, his sister. Even he knew that was a lie. It hadn't been only about helping his sister out since the moment he walked into that meeting at the country club and found Adeline hiding under the table.

The woman was sharp and snarky and sexy as hell, and maybe him doing this would help soften her a little. Riley inwardly groaned and reminded himself that this was the twenty-first century and not the eighteen-hundreds. As much as he'd like to be able to be the hero and help Adeline solve the case, the woman was incredibly talented and on a mission to prove that she didn't need a man. Maybe that's why she gave him a part in the plan that wasn't all that complicated. He only needed to talk to Greg about an upcoming proposal. Appeal to his need for more charitable and community work that would reflect well on him in advance of his upcoming election. Well, if Adeline didn't need him, then he needed to figure out how to make her want him.

Riley looked up, pulled from his thoughts of a fictional Adeline that was docile and needy, when a young, impeccably dressed man opened the inner chamber door.

"Mr. Thomas?"

Riley stood. "Yes?"

"Mayor Delaney will see you now."

"Thanks." Riley offered a tight smile to Greg's secretary and dipped into his brother-in-law's office.

"Riley how good to see you." Greg didn't stand, but he did plaster on his fake, wide smile. "Lance, can you fix us some scotch? Riley is Loren's brother."

Riley held up his hand, silently declining the drink, and Lance left without another word.

"Sorry to keep you waiting. You know how it is, always so busy. Seems like someone is always demanding my attention."

"No problem, but it did cut into my schedule, so I'll make it brief. Then, if you're interested, you can call me and we can try to set something else back up."

Greg raised his eyebrow, his curiosity clearly piqued. "Sounds interesting . . .go on."

"Okay, well, I'm not sure if you know this or not, but my grandparents left me some property, and I need a tax write-off. Business is going great, but with it comes exorbitant tax bills. I have two choices: pay the government or help those in need in our community. I figured that I'd like to help those in need."

"What do you have in mind?"

"Affordable housing."

"That sounds reasonable, but I don't understand how I can help with that."

"The city is holding me up on re-zoning, and when I was talking to Loren, she thought you might be able to help. Your involvement in the project would get you the kind of positive press you would be hard pressed to pass up, especially right before an election."

"Can you explain a little bit more?"

"My property is slated as agricultural and not commercial or residential. I know that the city has to acquire a certain number of government-sanctioned housing units per year. I was thinking I would build those homes, divide my land into residential parcels, and sell it to the city. Of course, I would agree to a lower sale price, since it's for the city, and I can always use it as a deduction." Riley made a mental note to call Loren and mention that if Greg asks, yes she and he had discussed this idea. "It would help me at the same time since I keep getting offers from Medical City, their offers are fair market value, but it would destroy me on taxes. This land is an inheritance. It's locked in a trust, so I haven't paid taxes on the value yet as an inheritance. But once I sell it—"

"You're screwed," Greg finished the sentence for him.

"Yep. I need to show a substantial loss, but as long as it is zoned agricultural, the value is low. If I can get it rezoned into a different class then the market value will skyrocket, which will make my donation of the land an even larger tax write-off."

"I'm glad that Loren said to talk with me, the woman really does know me. I have an idea of exactly what we can do. Let me clear the rest of my schedule for the day."

The man looked about ready to piss his pants with excitement and thrash himself for keeping Riley waiting.

"Sorry, but I can't stay today. I have a meeting, and I hate keeping clients waiting." Riley knew that it was petty, but he loved getting the upper hand. "Why don't you call me when your schedule is a bit more controllable?"

"Can't you reschedule whatever it is that you have?"

"Nope, call me crazy, but I still refuse to hire a secretary. It's a little more difficult for me to reschedule things. Thank you again for meeting me on such short notice, though."

"Absolutely, Riley, you're family. Hey, we're having a cocktail party this weekend, why don't you come? There will be several councilmen and other members of city committees present. It would be the perfect time for you to convince them we need the plot of land rezoned."

Riley wanted to roll his eyes. "Sounds good. Is this something I can bring a date to?"

"Absolutely." Greg's grin slipped for only a second before it was firmly back in place. "Loren hasn't mentioned you seeing someone."

"It's still new." They both stood and Riley reached out a hand, which Greg shook with the perfect, political grip. "Well, I'll see you at the party, if not before."

Riley left and gave himself a pat on the back because he knew he was leaving Greg salivating and wanting more. It wasn't exactly what Adeline had told him to do, but he'd improvised, and in the end, he believed that Adeline would be pleased. Feeling confident that Greg was probably calling that Hillary woman first, Riley dialed Loren as soon as he got into his truck.

"Hey, Ri."

"Only got a second but wanted to give you a heads-up. I met with Greg today."

"You what?" Loren half-squeaked, half-shouted into the phone.

"Listen to me, it's part of the plan. Anyway, Greg thinks I'm looking for some charitable tax deductions and considering selling my land that Gram and Gramps left me."

"You aren't, are you?"

"No, but he thinks I am. He also thinks that you and I discussed it and you advised me to talk with him about it since I might want to build affordable housing and it could help his campaign at the same time. He was very pleased with you by the way."

Loren let out a groan.

"Oh, and before I forget, he thinks that I have a girlfriend and will be bringing her to some dinner party this weekend."

"You have a girlfriend? What cocktail party?"

"Yes, Adeline is going to pretend that she is my girlfriend, and how did you not know about a cocktail party that you supposedly are throwing?"

"Great. I didn't know because obviously this is another of Greg's last-minute ideas that he thinks are no big deal because he is clueless about what all is involved. He thinks of no one but himself. I don't have time for this nonsense!"

"Sorry."

"Not your fault, Ri. By the way Adeline is the perfect girlfriend for you."

"You mean perfect fake girlfriend, this is just to help you."

"Okay, whatever you say. I'll let you know the details as soon as Greg tells me the details. Oh, and, Ri?"

"Yes?"

"You seem awful edgy when it comes to discussing Adeline."

"Shut up."

"Shutting up. Just saying. Okay, really, I'm shutting up now."

Riley disconnected and headed home because he didn't really have a meeting to get to.

When he walked in, he dropped his keys onto the counter, grabbed a Yuengling from the fridge and moved to the sliding glass doors that opened to the sprawling backyard. He didn't have to shout because as soon as he'd pulled up, Gerda, his German Shepherd, had recognized the sound of his truck and was already at the door waiting.

"Hey, girl, did you catch any criminals? Get some bite work in?" Gerda tilted her head and listened to him talk. For some reason, every German Shepherd Riley had owned since he was a kid had done that. Grinning, he headed back inside and collapsed onto the couch before flipping on the television. Gerda jumped up with him, taking up the two cushions to his left, and cut her eyes up to the episode of *Law and Order* he'd stopped on. Halfway through the episode, Riley's phone buzzed, and he shifted just enough to pull it from his pocket.

LOREN: Saturday evening. Grand Bohemian Hotel. Seven sharp. Black tie. Dinner is included. Cash bar. Greg said that he asked Lance to put you and Adeline at our table.

Riley: See you then.

HE HAD JUST MOVED to set his phone down when it rang with an unfamiliar number.

"Yesss?"

"Well, don't you sound like Suzie Sunshine?"

"Adeline?"

"Yep, the one and only, I was calling to talk about how your meeting went."

Riley let out a chuckle. "Hello, Adeline. Loren was getting ready to text you, did you get it?"

"Yes, she did. Awesome work, by the way. I was figuring we probably should meet and get our stories straight. Even if he doesn't suspect anything, Hillary will. Women tend to be more suspicious by nature."

"Sure, just tell me when."

"We only have three days, so is tomorrow good for you? I can meet any time."

"I can do early if you want to meet for coffee."

"I can do coffee just tell me where."

"Let's meet at Keke's downtown. How does seven sound?"

"In the morning?"

Okay at that Riley did laugh. "Yes, in the morning, is that too early?"

"But that means I have to get up at five thirty to get ready and be there on time. I'm not sure that I've ever been up at five thirty."

"Hold on." Riley tried to move Gerda, but she wasn't having it. "Gerda, I need to get up."

"Hey, Riley, no problem. Seven o'clock it is. See you then." Adeline hung up before Riley could say another word. He looked at the black screen, confusion pulling his brow together. All he wanted to do was go get his iPad so he could check his schedule for the morning and see if he could move their time to eight instead of seven. Sometimes, Adeline was too confusing.

Chapter Thirteen

RILEY

iley sat in his truck waiting for Adeline, but he wasn't overly confident that she would show. At two minutes after seven, he cut the engine and headed inside because whether she showed or not, he still needed coffee.

Keke's had two lines, one for those waiting for a seat and one for those waiting to place their order to go. He had just taken a step toward the to-go line when the door chimed and Adeline walked in. The woman looked freaking radiant. It was like one of those stupid chick-flick movies that his sister would watch when they were kids. The morning sun was casting a beam on Adeline, and it brought out the reddish hints to her hair. For some reason, he found red highlights almost as sexy as the skirt suit Adeline was wearing.

Riley shifted and told his cock to behave because sometimes that bastard had a mind of its own. "You're here?"

"You did say seven, right?" Adeline looked down at the Apple watch on her wrist. "It is exactly seven. Want to get a table?"

"Sure." Riley held out one arm and allowed Adeline to go

before him as the two moved to a back booth and then stayed standing until Adeline was seated. "Sorry that I had you meet me here so early, but I have a hectic afternoon."

"With Gerda?" Adeline said under her breath, but Riley heard it anyway. The abrupt hang up last night all made sense. She wasn't an ice queen, she was jealous, or at least she was like him; she felt something, that electricity between them, and she was fighting it.

"Well, no, I won't see Gerda until later when I get home."

"Oh, she lives with you?"

"Yes, she's lived with me for five years."

"And you haven't married her?" Adeline threw her hand over her mouth. "Sorry. That's none of my business."

"Umm, no, Gerda's nice to have around and all, but she isn't someone you marry." He hated himself just a bit, a very little bit, for yanking Adeline's chain, but it was the most fun he'd had in a while. To be honest, he'd had more fun since meeting Adeline, first at the WaWa, then the country club and now this. He was going to hell, he was sure of it, but at least he was having fun getting there.

"Anyway, let's get to business." Adeline was practically seething. "Here." She pulled a folder from her bag and tossed it onto the table.

Riley flipped through it. "Your dossier? Impressive."

"Wow, womanizer knows what a dossier is." Once again, Adeline's words were semi-muffled because she said them through clenched teeth. Riley lost it and started laughing. "What's so funny?" Riley didn't answer her because he was still laughing. "That is rude."

"Oh and calling someone a womanizer isn't?" He was still laughing when the server walked over to grab their order.

"Two black coffees?" Riley laughed as he ordered and then turned to Adeline. "Would you like some breakfast as well?"

Adeline turned to the server. "Make sure to bring lots of cream and sugar with those coffees, especially for his. Plus, I'll have one of your croissants with a side of fruit please."

Riley fought to hold back his smirk. He liked Adeline Morgan, and he liked her attitude even more. When the waitress walked off to place their order, he pulled out his phone and flipped through his photos until he found the perfect one. It was of him and Gerda on his boat out fishing. Gerda had her life vest on and was looking over the side of the boat, waiting for him to pull the line in. "Adeline, I think you have the wrong impression of me."

"And what impression is that? That you are like all other men?"

"Yeah . . . that one."

"What gives you that idea?"

Riley handed his phone over to Adeline, and she looked at the screen. "Cute dog."

"Yep. Her name is Gerda."

Adeline jerked her head up and then swung her eyes back to the screen. "Gerda is your dog?"

Riley nodded just as the waitress set the drinks and food onto their table.

"Anything else?"

"No, you can just leave the bill with me." Riley held out his hand but didn't look up as their server dropped the slip into his open palm before walking away. "Now that we have that cleared, can we move on?"

Adeline took a sip of coffee and then nodded.

"How long have the four of you worked—" Riley spoke at the same moment as Adeline.

"Just you and Loren—sorry, you go first."

"No you."

Adeline shook her head and shoved a large wad of croissant into her mouth prohibiting her from talking. Riley smiled. "Okay, I was just going to ask how long the four of you have worked together?"

"We actually met in college."

"What got you into the private investigating? Was it a family business?"

"Not a family business and it's sort of a long story."

"I have some time still." Riley didn't really, but dammit if he could get the blasted woman to open up, even just a little

"I find that admirable. But how do you find clients? Loren wouldn't tell me, she just had a card."

"That's how. Because of how involved we get, we can only take on a limited number of clients, so our business is purely based on referrals." Adeline held up one finger to let Riley know to hold that thought and stood from the booth. "Hey, chica."

Just that easily, Riley watched as the ice shield melted and a kind and gentle side of her appeared. She hugged the other woman, who was obviously a motorcycle deputy.

"Piper, this is Riley. Riley, this a good friend of ours and beloved helper to our cause, Piper." Riley stood and shook Piper's hand and then smiled as the newcomer gave Adeline a questioning look.

Adeline waved her off. "Yeah, he knows. Have time to sit?" Adeline scooted into the booth and made way for Piper.

"No, gotta run, but I saw you sitting over here and wanted to drop this off. Sunday sent me a text and asked me to look into a tag for her. Here's the info." Piper flipped open a small spiral notepad and pulled out a sheet of paper.

"Thank you."

Then, just as quickly as she appeared, Piper left, and Adeline returned to her normal, standoffish behavior that she seemed to reserve for him.

"Stop. Whatever questions you have brewing in that head

of yours, let's hold off on them, we need to focus on one thing at a time. Right now, it is coming up with our backstory so we have something to talk about when asked how we met, or how long we've been together, and what I do for a living." Pulling out her trusty notepad, Adeline flipped to a clean sheet of paper to take notes. "Is it just you and Loren? Any other siblings?"

"Nope, just the two of us."

"You two seem close."

"We are, but my family was always very close. Our dad left, couldn't take it."

"Couldn't take what?"

"My grandparents were hard workers and believed that everyone should be hard workers whether you needed to or not. My dad didn't agree. He was more of the mindset that once you could stop working, you should. He was lazy. He didn't like my grandparents riding his ass. We lived with my grandparents and they had no problem telling my dad to get a job and support his family. Gramps was always circling job openings in the papers for him, whether it be at IHOP or construction, but my dad kept saying that he went to school for business and wanted something in his field. That didn't sit well in our house. We all want something, but sometimes, we have to do things that we don't like until we can get what we want, it's called paying our dues."

"Tell me to mind my own business if you want to, but if your dad wasn't a fan of working and your grandfather drove a truck . . ."

"How did we end up with family money?"

Adeline nodded as she shoved a large piece of flaky crois-sant into her mouth.

"My grandparents invested every penny they had in land and penny stock."

"Penny stock? Like what?"

"Tupperware and Darden Restaurants." Riley's face turned slightly red with embarrassment as he announced these, not because his family was wise enough to invest, but because he didn't want to sound as if he was bragging.

"But it takes some serious capital to develop shopping and medical plazas?" Adeline sounded like she was genuinely interested, so Riley decided to tell her even more.

"For over one hundred years the Thomas family has lived in Central Florida. Some people said they were stupid for investing so much of their money into property, especially when they were buying swamp land. But people stopped laughing when a man named Walt bought a large portion of their land to build a theme park dedicated to a mouse. It sort of set me up to do whatever I wanted to do."

Adeline choked on the croissant she'd just popped into her mouth. "I guess so."

"Okay . . . going on . . ." Adeline smiled. "I'm really admiring your family right now. I think that I'd like your grandparents. They sound like awesome people."

"They were."

"Oh, I'm sorry."

"My grandparents came across hard, but they doled out love by the buckets. My mom was diagnosed with renal cell cancer my senior year of high school, Loren was in sixth grade. My mom held on for four years, but her death was hard on all of us, especially my grandparents. I'd never seen them break down. I think we are naturally programmed to adjust to the loss of a parent because it is the way of life. But for parents, I don't think they are programmed to deal with losing a child. We lost Grams almost two years later to the date, and Gramps was devastated, he wanted to go after that. He was gone less than a year later." Riley felt it, he hadn't noticed it while he'd been lost in his memories, but at some point, Adeline had reached out and wrapped her hand around his. "Enough about me, what about you?"

"All of my stuff is in that dossier, let me ask a few more. Where do you live? What exactly do you do? And is Gerda your only pet?"

"I live out toward Lake Nona, and I own my own home. Yes, she's my only pet, but don't call her that, she thinks she is a human. And as for a job, I'm a contractor. Basically, I buy land and then develop it for various projects. Sometimes, it's shopping centers, and sometimes, it's residential. If it is going to be a shopping area, then I work with architects, landscapers, and surveyors to get it going. Basically, I'm the money man, the idea guy." Riley took a sip of coffee. "By the way, I think your idea of using my goal to get the land rezoned was genius. Sounds bad, but in the end, he might actually do me a favor."

"That's a good thing, right? By the way, when was your last girlfriend?" Adeline blushed, realizing that her question sounded very intrusive. "So we can establish a timeline, you know, for how long we've been dating. I don't want to say two months and then find out that last month you were with another woman and Greg totally knew that."

"Greg knows very little about me. I go over there to see my sister and niece about twice a week, and he's almost never there. But, to answer the question, I haven't had a girlfriend in a while, so two months will be fine."

Riley was playing it cool, but it had been almost two years since he and Sarah had broken up. She was sweet but had higher aspirations than Riley did.

"Got it." Adeline wrote it down in her notepad. "I find that it's better to stay as close to the truth as possible, so I use my real name, but when people ask me what I do for a living, I just tell them that I work at an outreach program. You would be shocked to know how many people change the topic as quickly as they can after that. As far as background, don't worry, I have all the credentials to back up my story, including an established website, thanks to Sunday."

"You four really cover all the bases, huh?"

Adeline leaned in. "You have no idea. Sunday is downright scary sometimes." She chuckled. "Okay, we got this. Thank you for meeting me."

"Thank you for meeting me so early. I'll remember next time that you aren't a morning person." Adeline looked sheepish, but they both knew that he'd spoken truth. "Is your address in this file folder?" Riley opened it and flipped to scan the papers.

"Yes," Adeline answered. "I live downtown."

"Well, the cocktail party is at the Bohemian, why don't I pick you up at six thirty? We can have a drink beforehand."

"Sounds good." Adeline stood, and Riley quickly pulled a few twenties from his wallet. He was leaving a generous amount on the table, but he didn't want to wait, he wanted to walk out with Adeline. Hurrying to catch up with her, he walked in sync with her steps to her car.

"There's that car, I bet it belongs to some kid who doesn't know how to listen to his music . . ."

"Below eighty-five decibels," they both said the last part in unison.

"Listen, Adeline, I am sorry for the way we met. I'm not usually such a . . ."

"Dick?"

"Yeah."

"You're forgiven. Don't be too hard on yourself, though. I shock the shit out of most people, especially when they actually get a good look at me. Somehow the skirt fools them into thinking that I'd be driving an Audi. But, shhh . . .I'm more badass than they know." Adeline unlocked her car. Before she got in, Riley moved in closer and brushed her hair back. He tucked it behind her ear. "Yes, totally badass." Then he did something that he'd been wanting to do, he kissed her. Not deep or invasive but sweet and fast. Just enough to make Adeline want more and to remember the feel of his lips the rest of the day.

Chapter Fourteen

ADELINE

*I*t didn't matter that five years separated Adeline and Sunday, or that Melanie and Olivia fell somewhere closer in age to Sunday than they did her. When it came to things like this, they were all little girls.

"Wear this one." Melanie pulled out Adeline's black Tom Ford evening gown with the illusion panel from her closet. "It will have Riley groveling at your feet."

"Yes, that one is gorgeous on you," Sunday agreed as she twisted Adeline's hair up into an elegant chignon.

Melanie turned the gown around so everyone could see it. "Made in China?" Melanie lifted the tag. "Have you ever wondered if clothes in China say made around the corner?"

"No. You want to know what I wonder about?" Sunday pointed to the bag of chips sitting on the vanity that they were all picking from. "How can Doritos have a date"—she pointed to the expiration—"and the rest of us don't?" Sunday shoved a chip in her mouth before picking up a bobby pin and shoving it into Adeline's hair. "Or why can't, just once, a bag say, serving size: you're good boo, eat as much you want?"

"What are you complaining about Sunday, I'm the

chunkiest one out of all of us?" Adeline looked at herself in the mirror, not for the first time feeling a little self-conscious.

"Anyway, onto other topics, I slipped a few condoms into your purse, just in case." Olivia winked.

"Just in case I grow a dick?" Adeline couldn't help herself.

"No, just in case he isn't prepared and you two can't wait until you get somewhere to buy some."

Adeline shook her head. "There are so many things wrong with that statement. I'm just going to let it go."

They were busy trying to get Adeline ready for the party and all she could do was think about that kiss from the other day. For three days, it had been at the forefront of her mind. She'd wanted more, she'd wanted to wrap her hands around the back of his neck and pull him closer. God, she was such a hussy. Adeline laughed because that was one thing she definitely wasn't, so thinking it was absurd. She'd met several women her age that already had three, four, or even five kids. Unfortunately, a few weren't sure who the correct baby-daddies were. Adeline swore right then and there that if she could match her shoes to her outfit then, damn it, she better always be able to match her babies to their daddy—even if that meant abstinence at times.

"Did Olivia tell you what she did today?" Sunday tapped Olivia's arm with the hairbrush, teasing Adeline about something that she'd clearly missed. "Go ahead, tell her. I think that we should all use it as a standard line."

"Just tell me," Adeline groaned, but Melanie was already laughing.

"Some lady called the office and immediately started in on our prices, asking us how much it would be if she just wanted proof her husband was cheating but didn't want to divorce him."

"Good god, did you tell her that we weren't her husband's babysitter? Hell, I'd charge her more just for being an idiot."

"No, I told her that if she really wanted to know, she could find out for free."

Adeline was curious, but at the same time, she was scared about what Olivia was going to say next because Sunday and Melanie were cackling.

"I told her to take his cell phone from him, run to the bathroom, and lock the door, if he chases after her and tries to get it, then he's cheating. If he doesn't care, then he's a good man."

Adeline had to hold her fingers under her eyes to keep her mascara from smearing as she laughed.

"You better hurry." Sunday stepped away from Adeline and put the hairbrush down, clearly finished with her masterpiece. "Ignore Livi, Riley is a client just as much as Loren is, and you're there to get cozy with Greg. We need to find that missing piece, something is fucking missing, and it is driving me nuts."

"You mean something other than that he's having an affair with a married woman, who he's known since college and started a business with back at said college, and is selling his wife's land without his wife's knowledge to said company for a fraction of its value then turning around and selling it to the city for an enormous profit? You mean besides that?" Olivia was clearly perturbed.

"It's all hearsay without legal proof." Melanie knew how to fire us up, that fucking word, *hearsay*. It was probably Adeline's least favorite word in the entire English language. It wasn't hearsay, they knew all this for fact, but they needed more than a few fuzzy pictures, a horrendous audio recording, and a forged signature on a quick claim.

"I'll get the proof, I promise." Adeline stood and walked over to her closet door where Olivia had hung the dress. She slipped it on and then turned around for someone to zip her up. When she turned again, all three ladies let out a chorus of wolf whistles.

"Hot as hell," Melanie whispered.

"Chill, this isn't a real date, remember? This is for work."

"Whatever you say." Melanie rolled her eyes. "But I'm not buying whatever it is that you're trying to convince us of. I've seen the way you look at him. I can tell there's something between the two of you whether you're ready to admit it or not."

"Don't forget the protection," Olivia hollered.

"You saw me attach my holster." Adeline misunderstood Olivia on purpose.

"You know what I meant."

"Yep, and I'm still not acknowledging it."

"I think he's here." Sunday ran over to peer out Adeline's window. "Yep, just pulled up." Melanie, Olivia, and Sunday headed out, and Adeline gave herself one final look over in the mirror before moving into the living room.

Taking several deep breaths, she opened the door just as he rang the bell, and she was glad she had gotten her breathing in order. If she hadn't, it was very likely she would have started hyperventilating. There was nothing sexier than a man in a penguin suit. His black tuxedo was expertly tailored, and Adeline loved that he was wearing a tie instead of a bowtie with a vest. It made him look much more fashionable.

"Adeline." She felt a tap on her back and turned to see Melanie standing behind her. "Would you like me to put those in water for you?"

Adeline looked back at Riley, totally lost. Put what in water? What in the hell was Melanie talking about? Then she saw that he was holding a bouquet of long-stem white roses. "Oh my, those are lovely, thank you." She gratefully accepted them, drinking in their fragrance one time before turning and handing them to Melanie. "I would appreciate that."

Then she turned and allowed Riley to escort her out to a Cadillac CT6. "Where's your truck?"

"I figured that it might be difficult to hop up in a dress, so I pulled out the Cadi. You look exquisite, by the way." Adeline shivered as Riley's words mixed with his warm breath brushed along her neck a second before he was helping her slide into the car.

As Riley drove, he kept one hand on the steering wheel and one hand resting face-up on the center console. Adeline kept staring down at muscular hand. It was like an invitation, asking her to trust him...give him her hand.

*R*iley opened the door and held out one hand. For the first time in his life, he felt like a real-life fucking Prince Charming as he assisted Adeline out of the car before heading toward the doors of the Bohemian. Riley rolled his eyes at the pomp and circumstance for the evening: ropes, carpet, and uniformed guards, not to mention valets to park the cars when there was plenty of parking less than twenty feet away. Handing his keys off, he hurried over and placed a hand on the back of Adeline and they were stopped by the flash of a camera.

"I can't believe Loren pulled it all together so fast."
"Name?"

"Name?" A woman holding a clipboard asked them.

Riley looked up and saw Lance, Greg's assistant, hurtling toward them. "This is the mayor's brother-in-law, move," Lance snapped, basically elbowing the woman out of the way to lead Riley and Adeline inside.

Adeline had to walk double-time just to keep up as Lance maneuvered through the crowd. Riley decided that now was the perfect time to lose the rude asshole, so he tightened his grip on Adeline's hand and pulled her back to him, slowing his pace until Lance was long gone.

"You're here." Riley and Adeline looked up to see Loren stepping toward them. She was holding a glass of champagne and wearing a pale pink evening gown.

"Hey, sis." Riley leaned down and placed a kiss on Loren's cheek. "We were just admiring how fast you throw a party together."

"Remind me later how much I hate the two of you for this, I haven't slept in days."

"Adeline, you look beautiful. My god that dress, it was made for you." Loren gave her a hug, which Adeline returned, and something about their camaraderie warmed Riley. He liked seeing his sister and this woman . . . Adeline . . . his ex-sparring partner, get along.

"Thank you, Loren, you look amazing yourself. Your gown is stunning."

"Greg said that he's very excited to spend time with the two of you." Loren used air quotes when she said excited.

Chapter Sixteen

ADELINE

*A*deline felt a little out of place next to Loren. Sure, she could hold her own in the snobbiest of get-togethers, but Loren wasn't snobby, she was sweet and classy. Whereas Adeline resembled a female trucker more than she did the demure housewife. Adeline told herself that this was just one of the many reasons why she and Riley could never be a *we, she could never fit in with his crowd, his family.*

"Uh-oh. He has just spied you two, he's headed over," Loren warned, interrupting Adeline's self-examination.

"Riley, so good to see you." Greg gave a half-handshake, half-hug. "Who do we have here?"

When the mayor stepped back and had to tilt his head, Adeline gave him her most charming smile and waited.

"Greg, I'd like you to meet Adeline Morgan, my girlfriend. Adeline, this is Greg, Loren's husband."

Adeline was giving Riley a mental high-five for his little dig of not using his name nor his official title. It was nice to remind people who thought they were all that and a bag of chips that they were normal human beings. Yeah, asshole, we are really here for Loren, you are just the by-product.

"Nice to meet you, Mr. Delaney." Adeline held out her hand to Greg.

"Oh, call me Greg. We are all family here." Adeline had to fight back a laugh when she saw Riley roll his eyes. "Why don't we let the ladies talk? There are several people I'd like to introduce you to." Greg waited for Riley's response, but Riley didn't budge.

Adeline nodded. "Go. Loren and I can get to know each other better."

"Sweetheart"—Greg reached for Loren's hand and placed a kiss on it—"why don't you take Adeline around and introduce her to some of the other ladies. We will meet you two at the table in a few for dinner." Greg started to walk off, but Riley was still watching her to make sure she was okay. Adeline nodded once more to assure Riley that she was fine. She was still close enough that she could overhear their conversation, and thank god Loren caught on because she helped strategically move them to the aid in their proximity.

Greg's voice was low, but Adeline could still hear him. "I was just telling them about your idea for affordable housing. Do you know Councilman Chatham?" Adeline's heart raced at the name, she wanted to turn around and see.

"Can't say that I do."

"Dan, this is my brother-in-law, Riley Thomas, he owns RT Land. It's a development company."

Shit. Adeline was fidgeting, was Hillary here as well?

For the next ten minutes Adeline had to keep tuning out Greg and Riley to chat with random women who wanted nothing other than to talk. Adeline had never been one for small talk, in fact, she found it tedious and unnecessary. She had never understood why people felt the need to talk just to talk. What was wrong with being quiet? Well, she thought it was mundane until she heard the name Sienna Miller.

Adeline held her hand and got the weirdest vibe. The

woman standing across from her was brunette, curvy, not quite as tall, and wearing a black gown.

"You two could be sisters," Loren added in sweetly and innocently.

"So, Sienna, do you work with the mayor?"

"I do. I'm an intern."

"How fun, do you like it?" Adeline didn't really need to ask. She could tell just by the look on the woman's face that she hated working for Greg. So, Adeline waited until Loren was talking to someone else and then whispered. "He seems so smarmy to me." She gave a head tilt toward Greg. Sienna's shoulders relaxed, the tiniest smile cracked her face, and the roll of her eyes told Adeline that Sienna was giving a silent agreement. "Are there many interns at City Hall?"

"Right now it's just me, but there will be another one soon, I'm sure. We seldom go with just one."

"Oh. Loren had mentioned that interns worked there for two years. How much more do you have to go?"

"Fourteen months and three days."

"You're counting, you must be excited to get out and start the next chapter of your life."

"Yep, that's it. Happy to get out and—"

"Dinner is about to be served." Adeline turned and saw Lance standing just behind them, he must have first whispered to Greg *sotto voce,* before coming over to Loren.

"You heard the man, let's go into dinner." Greg started walking toward the main dining room, not waiting for Adeline and Loren to catch up or turning around to notice that they were just behind him.

"You and Adeline, you two serious?"

"You mean are we talking marriage? No. We've been together two months. It's all still new."

"She's one fine piece of ass."

Loren squeezed Adeline's hand at those words.

"Those kinds of women are nice candy, but you don't marry them. Keep them around, play with them, but don't marry them. I wouldn't be shocked if half the men in this room have been with her, she just has that look, you know? Don't get me wrong, it's a good look, a real good look."

Riley clenched his fist as Greg spoke. "I think you've misread Adeline, she's a counselor, she works with women that have been mistreated."

Greg let out a condescending chuckle. "If you say so, okay."

"Adeline, I'm so sorry." Loren's words finally reached the two men in front of them and they both turned, Riley's face was pinched, but Greg looked completely at ease and unapologetic.

"It's okay, don't worry about it. Can't believe everything everyone says, can we?" Adeline peeked down at Greg's crotch, and Riley fought the urge to chuckle. She felt Loren's hand tighten around hers.

Greg turned and marched on in to the room.

"Holy shit, Adeline." Loren let out a low whistle. "Truly, though, I'm sorry about what he said."

"Loren, go on inside, we'll be there in a few minutes." Riley stepped out of the way of people walking and pulled Adeline along with him. "I'm sorry. The man is an asshole. We can leave if you want to. Or, I can go kick his ass if you want. The only reason I didn't before was because I was worried you'd be pissed if I ruined the plan."

"Are you kidding? If I wanted that, I'd kick his ass myself."

"Yes, you will, tough girl." Riley wrapped one arm and tucked her close as he led her to their seats, which were right next to Loren and Greg. Also at their table was Councilman Dan Chatham, but Hillary was nowhere to be seen.

"Where's Hillary tonight, Dan? I don't think she's ever missed one of Greg's events?"

"She had a really bad migraine." He sounded genuinely concerned.

"Does she suffer from them often?" Adeline asked.

"No. I don't remember her ever having one before, but she said her head was killing her. And Loren is right, Hillary never misses an event, so that told me that she was truly sick."

"Well, tell her that we missed her." Loren was genuinely concerned because she had no clue.

Adeline scanned the room as they ate, trying to casually take in every face. It didn't take her long to nudge Riley's elbow.

"Riley," Adeline whispered.

He leaned over to her.

"Check out the man at three o'clock by the exit door."

"Yep, already noticed him. There's one more directly behind you."

"Can you tell me why a mayor needs armed bodyguards? This is his dinner."

"No clue. Need to find out if this is the norm. Are you ready to get out of here?"

The idea was music to her ears. She'd been ready for over an hour. Hell, she'd been ready since they pulled up in front of the Bohemian earlier tonight.

"Adeline?"

"Yes?"

"Once we get through all of this and I don't have to play nice with Greg for you or for my sister, I'm going to cold-cock that son-of-a-bitch. No one and I mean no one will ever talk about you like that again, at least not within my earshot."

Chapter Seventeen

ADELINE

*A*deline was getting frustrated and so was everyone else; it had been two weeks since she went to dinner at the Bohemian and still nothing. Adeline and Riley had been invited over to the Delaney's home twice, and both times, Riley had mentioned being shocked that Greg had actually stayed home. But still they hadn't been able to get a good hold, discover how they were going to ruin this man, or blow the case open for all to know what a dirtbag he was.

Adeline reached into her bag and pulled out her phone. "Hello?"

"Hey gorgeous, what are you doing? Got time for lunch?"

"I can make time, what do you have in mind?" Riley calling her midday and asking her to lunch had happened two other times since the dinner, and both times, she felt the same as she did then. Giddy. There was something so sweet and romantic about it.

"Greg just called and wants me to meet him and a business associate . . . are you ready for this?"

Adeline's excitement faded, this was business not wooing.

"The business associate is named Trinity Reynolds."

"Holy shit, I'm ready. Want me to meet you there? Just tell me when and where."

"I'm actually on my way to your office now to get you."

Adeline glanced at the clock, which read just after eleven thirty. "How far away are you?" She looked to her left as the elevator dinged and out walked Riley with the phone still up to his ear.

"I'm not far at all." He smiled his adorable grin.

Adeline hung up and grabbed her purse. "I'll be back. We are having lunch with Greg and someone named Trinity Reynolds."

"No shit?" Olivia practically shouted. "As in Hillary Trinity Reynolds?"

"Do you think Hillary would be bold enough to show up?" Melanie asked.

Adeline shrugged, having no true way of knowing. Sunday was up and moving toward their backroom. Less than five minutes later, she was back with two small jewelry boxes. Adeline recognized them, and didn't hesitate to swap the earrings she was wearing with the ones Sunday handed her. When she attached the back on one of them an almost transparent wire came up from the back of her ear and then slid into her ear unnoticed. Then, Adeline opened the second box, which held a pretty but unassuming necklace, and fastened the chain around her neck.

Arching one brow, Riley's lips were quirked as he attempted to work out what he was seeing.

"Microphones so that the girls can hear everything I hear, and the wire just in case there's an emergency and they need to get ahold of me. Necklace is a camera, same thing, they can see what I see."

"But the earrings are black?"

"Sort of like two-way mirrors," Adeline explained as she

slid out her desk drawer, pulled out a box of ammo and tossed it into her purse.

Riley shook his head and decidedly didn't ask any more questions.

"Be safe," Melanie hollered as the two of them got onto the elevator, Riley's arm wrapped protectively around Adeline's waist, and they headed down.

They arrived at Cooper's Hawk, a nice steakhouse in the tourist area that many locals avoid, especially during the day when all the parks were open. Adeline made a mental note of Greg's location planning.

When they walked in, they were notified that the mayor was already there and were escorted to a table where he sat with a woman who was clearly not Hillary Chatham.

"Riley, Adeline, I'd like you to meet Trinity Reynolds. Trinity, this is my brother and his friend."

"Brother-in-law and my girlfriend," Riley corrected.

"Nice to meet you both, Greg has told me much about you."

Adeline stared at Trinity, clearly confused and hoping that Sunday was working her magic. The woman had to be younger than Adeline by at least ten years. Riley pulled out Adeline's chair and waited for her to sit before scooting it closer to the table.

"So Trinity, what is it that you do?" Adeline got right to the questions so that Sunday and the girls could start their research. But Trinity didn't look at Adeline when she asked. She was too busy looking at Greg with lovesick puppy eyes.

"Do you see what I see?" someone whispered into Adeline's ear. It was whispered so she couldn't quite tell who had spoken the words, but she thought it was Olivia. "At Greg's six o'clock, is that a bodyguard?"

Adeline pressed back into her chair and tried to look

around Greg to see, yep, it was the same guy she'd spied the other night.

"Mhmm," Adeline answered nonchalantly. "Trinity?"

The woman didn't look. Adeline shook her head, if Greg was going to get someone to pretend to be Trinity Reynolds, the least he could do was have her practice answering to the damn name. Adeline cleared her throat and gave Riley a wry smile. "Trinity," she said a bit louder. There was a bump under the table, and Adeline fought to hold back the laugh. At least someone recognized the name, and he'd alerted his actress to answer.

"I'm sorry, my mind was somewhere else."

"No problem. I asked if you worked at City Hall as well?"

"No, I own a small real estate company. In fact, we handle a lot of deals for the city, which is why Greg asked me to come."

"Yes, yes. I invited Trinity since Riley and I had business to discuss. I didn't know that he was going to bring you, Adeline."

"I'm sorry, I can call a taxi." Adeline pushed her chair back, and Greg didn't say a word.

"No, you're not." Riley placed a hand on hers.

"Maybe that would be best, Riley, so we can talk business," Greg suggested.

"I invited Adeline because she knows all about my ideas for the project and actually has been helping me in my office in her free time. If you feel that it is best to discuss this another time, then she and I can go." Riley started to stand.

"Oh no, I just had no clue that the two of you had become so close, or that she knew so much about your business." Greg gave Trinity a look and then smiled. "Let's order lunch and then we can talk business."

"He isn't happy that you're there," the voice said into

Adeline's ear. She fought to mask her smile. She liked knowing that her friends were there with her.

They ordered and Greg immediately set in on his spiel. "Trinity often acts as a liaison for us. Especially for things like this."

"What do you mean?" Riley took a bite of his lunch and looked over at Trinity to see if she was following along or lost in space. She came across a tad ditzy.

"We're family, and there is a reason people say not to mix business and family. Her company acts as a holding company, they buy the property from you at the agreed upon price and then sell it to the city, so we don't have anyone claiming nepotism."

"But I was selling it to the city for practically nothing." Riley could smell a rat a mile away, and Greg was a rat, he was up to something. Probably the same thing he was up to with Loren's property. He would sell it to the city for twenty times more.

"Honey," Adeline said, "why don't you just transfer it to me and I'll sell it to the city? That way, we don't have that nepotism connection at all."

Greg looked sick to his stomach. "Well, that isn't how things work. It isn't that easy."

Adeline tilted her head to listen and gave Greg her innocent smile as she batted her eyelashes and played poor, stupid, little female. "You and Riley are still a couple, people saw you together at the dinner. Plus, Trinity is a real estate business, it is a much more professional way to do things and it removes all of us."

Adeline, refusing to be beaten, smiled widely at Greg and then reached under the table and slid her hand onto Riley's leg. "Ri, didn't you say that you were seriously considering just donating the property? Why not avoid all of the hassle and just do that? You'll get the larger deduction on your taxes.

I'm sure the city will gladly accept a donation of land, especially when it is slated for affordable housing. I can get a few of my friends who work for local news stations and the newspaper and have them run stories about the land donation and how it is going to be used."

"What friends at local news stations and the newspaper?" the mystery voice said into Adeline's ear.

"Addy, that's a great idea." Riley placed his hand on hers and held it firmly in place against his strong thigh.

"Let me see how that works," Greg sputtered.

"It's easy, I looked into it years ago when I wanted to start a women's shelter." Adeline dismissed Greg as though he knew very little about how things worked.

"But . . . but things work differently today."

There was nothing that Adeline liked less than a weak man. Greg Delaney liked to pretend he was strong, but he was a weak-ass bitch.

"I think that Addy . . ." There it was again, that nickname, a name no one had called her since she was a kid, a name that only Sasha had called her. She had hated it since, but coming from Riley, it sounded endearing. Like he saw her differently than everyone else did. It was almost as if he didn't see her tough-girl persona, instead he saw her as someone sweet, someone worth protecting, someone worth loving. "Had a great idea. Why don't you look into a donation? I could really use the tax write-off. This way, we won't have to go through all the legal red tape of transferring ownership from me to Trinity and then from Trinity to the city."

"I will look into this, but I don't think it is a smart idea. Loren told you to trust me, believe me, I understand how all of this works much better than your girlfriend does."

Adeline jerked back, not because of Greg's words, but because Riley tensed his hands and squeezed the ever-loving-shit out of Adeline's fingers without knowing his own strength. "If you'll excuse me for a second." Adeline stood and went to the restroom.

"Sunday can you hear me?"

"Yes, what's going on?"

"I'm going to take one of my earrings out and leave it on the table. Can one of you head over to Cooper's Hawk and pick it up? As soon as you hear them leaving, call and tell them you left the earring so they can hold it at the front hostess stand. But I want Riley and I to follow them. Let me know what they say."

"Will do."

Adeline removed the earring without the mic and cupped it in her hand. Fluffing her hair, she brought the left side forward to hide the fact that she was missing an earring.

She took a seat, expecting to have to make some excuse, but Riley was ready to go. She took one last sip of her soda, wiped her mouth with her napkin, and set her earring and napkin on the table.

Riley walked out of the restaurant, his arm around Adeline a little tighter than when they walked in. Something about Greg's dismissal of her made him protective, and something about the way he touched her had made her want more.

"They're talking," a voice said into Adeline's ear.

"I left one of my earrings on the table. The girls are listening to what is being said. How much of a hurry are you in?"

"You are scary."

Adeline grinned.

"Not in a hurry. I have the rest of the day."

"Let's see what they're up to." Adeline and Riley got into his truck and moved to the next parking lot, where they still had a clear view of the front doors of the restaurant.

"Holy shit, Adeline, you are missing it."

"What? What am I missing Livi?"

"Greg is pissed that you were there, he hates you. He's pissed that Heather, I guess that's her real name, wasn't more active in persuading Riley to use her realty service. But Heather is trying to explain that she doesn't know anything about real estate in the first place. I guess Greg wanted her to convince him to just sell it for a minimal amount so he could deduct all the land value and Greg could sell it to the city and he and Heather have the profit."

"Shit." Melanie cut in. "I think the man is either pulling the wool over Hillary and Heather's eyes or he's trying to set up homes with each of them. Maybe he's really a polygamist?"

"Well, that would fuel the rumor mill." Olivia went back to recounting the events. "She sounds like she is about to throw some epic temper tantrum and Greg is trying to calm her down."

Adeline quickly relayed what was going on to Riley.

"Oh, shit, they're coming out. They are dropping the words *fuck* and *cock* a lot, so there is about to be some serious business going on."

"There they are." Riley pointed.

"Yep." Adeline didn't know how to tell him what the girls had just relayed.

"What's wrong, Addy?"

She bit back a smile and whispered, "He and that woman are having an affair, and from their last bit of conversation, they are getting ready to continue their affair."

"Motherfucker," Riley seethed.

They watched as Heather walked out of the restaurant. She got into the backseat of a large car with extremely dark tinted windows. A few minutes later, Greg walked out and got into the same car's backseat. Riley started his engine, ready to follow, but Adeline stopped him.

"Holy shit, are they going to make out in the parking lot?

Go, Adeline, go up to the car and hold the necklace up to the window." The voice was loud and clearly Sunday's.

"But the windows are dark tinted. "You'll still be able to see something, and then when they finally come out, we'll be able to piece it all together."

Adeline put her hand on the door, but Riley reached over to stop her. "Whoa, wait a minute, where do you think you're going?"

"I want to know if we can see anything though the windows." She reached up and removed her necklace.

"Not without me you aren't."

"Fine come with me." Adeline pushed the door open, and Riley was right behind her, sliding across the seat and out onto her side. Holding the pendant, she walked toward the car and tried to move so that she was constantly looking away. She came from around the back and up to the side, crouched, and then pressed the pendant of the necklace against the glass.

"Holy shit, Adeline. Your mic is picking up everything. We're recording. Don't talk." One of the girls whispered, so Adeline pressed her finger against her lips to signal to Riley to do the same. "Bingo, we got it. Oh yeah, you can see perfectly clearly that it is Mayor Delaney and that he is wearing a wedding band." Adeline's heart broke just a bit at those words. She wasn't sure why, since she knew Greg was a pig, but she always held out hope.

With the affair clearly in the bag, Adeline decided that she might as well go pick up her earring. After waddling away from the car until both she and Riley were in the clear, she handed the necklace to him. "Here, you stay in front and hold this, maybe he'll crawl out half-dressed. I'll go in and pick up my earring."

"Olivia is on her way," Melanie chimed into her earpiece.

"Got it."

She should have felt good about finding the evidence they needed, but really, it made her kind of sad. This just meant they were one step closer to the end of the case. Deep down, Adeline knew the real problem: once the case was over, Riley would be gone. There'd be no more need for him to call her or take her out, and she really enjoyed being with him, even though he'd only kissed her that one time.

She picked up her earring from the hostess and walked out just as Olivia pulled up into a parking spot. "Didn't Melanie call you?"

"Shit, I was driving so I didn't answer."

"We were still here, so I told her to let you know that I'd grab it. But since you're here, you might as well give me a ride back to the office and save Riley a trip."

"I don't mind." Riley reached for Adeline, but she stepped toward Olivia's car.

"Are you sure, Adeline? I've got a few errands to run."

"I'm sure, it will save him the trip. We've inconvenienced him enough by having him help with the case."

"I didn't mind, really." He placed a hand on the passenger door of Olivia's car before Adeline could open it and cupped her face, pulling her toward him. "I don't know what you're playing at, but if you're trying to play hard to get, don't worry, you're worth playing for." He leaned forward and placed a gentle kiss at the edge of Adeline's lips and then opened her car door.

Chapter Eighteen
ADELINE

*A*deline was throwing her hands up in the air shouting as she stood next to Sunday, "I don't fucking care. You all saw the guy at lunch, well, at dinner it was him plus another goon. If it hadn't been for the fact that Greg had sent his bodyguard off on some fool's errand before he got into the car, then we would be busted, if not worse...in a gun fight. We need to fucking up our game." Adeline took a deep breath and tried to regain her composure. After all, it wasn't Sunday that she was mad at. "What did you find Sunday? Do all mayors have bodyguards?"

"I don't know about all mayors, but Orlando's never has, from what I can find."

"See? We need to pay closer attention, move in pairs until this is over. I'm headed to Max's, anyone want to go with me?"

The Maximum Guns and Ammunition shop had become a frequent hangout for the girls. As a retired deputy, Max, the owner, knew everyone, and he was someone the girls trusted. Not to mention one of the few people who knew the truth about their job.

Adeline counted her blessings often, and one of them was Max, the owner of the gun shop. He had been on shift the night Adeline had gotten pulled over for speeding. When she confessed to having a gun in the glove box, he was impressed. One, because she had it stored properly, and two, because she appeared confident and knowledgeable when she answered his questions about the gun. After that night, the girls all started going to Maximum Guns. He trained them in defensive tactics and grappling, and he also supplied them with the latest tools for their trade.

They had been newbies at the time, Melanie at least had *some* experience shooting. She had followed her father plenty of times to the shooting range when she was younger. But it was Olivia who shocked them all. She had mad skills, a natural sharpshooter. She never missed a target, even blindfolded. She just listened to the sounds. She'd fire once, and by the echo of the impact, she naturally knew how to adjust. It didn't take long for Olivia to be teased as their go-to marksman . . . markswoman, if they ever needed a markswoman.

Adeline, who was the first to arrive, hightailed it from the car and headed toward the door with her duffle in hand, storming the gun shop through the bulletproof glass just as the others pulled into the parking lot.

"Hey, Max, how's it hanging?"

"Good god, Adeline, that is crass." He grinned. "I was wondering when I'd see you four."

"Well, here we are," Olivia said as she and the others strode through the door.

"What can I do for ya? Here for practice or something else?"

Adeline glanced over her shoulder to get a quick look at how many people were in the shooting area. Faint sounds of gunfire could be heard echoing from within the protective glass enclosure that was divided into eight sections.

"We're here for practice." Olivia slapped a wad of money onto the counter.

"Must have a new case, eh?" Max slowly slid the money toward his side of the counter and dropped it into the till. "Hey, I just got this beaut in, you need to try it, Olivia. Got quite a kick, but the accuracy is spot on." He handed the snub-nose revolver over and Olivia balanced it in her hand, feeling the weight. "Only a five shot . . ."

"Yeah, but you only need one," Olivia and Max said in unison.

"Okay, if you two will stop with the love affair over the gun, let's practice." Adeline picked up a cardboard target, walked to the changing area, and set her duffle bag inside one of the lockers. Then she pulled out her earplugs and padded ear guards. She slipped those on, then pulled out her 9mm Smith and Wesson, a box of ammunition, and her shatterproof eyeglasses out before she closed the locker. Just to the left of the small storage area were two soundproof doors. They all had to enter through the first one together and wait for it to close before opening the second one. It ensured that no loud noises or ill-aimed bullets made their way out into the customer area.

As they walked down the row to four empty stations, Adeline mentally clocked the tourist who were happy to be in a state—or country, for that matter— that allowed guns. Because if the shock over getting to shoot wasn't enough for the male visitors, then seeing four women dressed in heels and dresses definitely did it.

"Poor babies are going to be shown up," Adeline whispered around a smile. "We'll make sure that Olivia goes first. That will probably make them clear the area fast."

Placing their targets on hooks on a slide belt, they each

pressed a button on their stand and slid the target back, letting their targets slide past the five, ten, fifteen, and didn't stop until they hit fifty yards. Taking one step back, Adeline looked around the divider wall and smiled, meeting the eyes of Olivia, Sunday, and Melanie.

Olivia loaded her Glock, fired, and hit the bull's-eye.

Sunday loaded her Beretta 9mm, fired, and hit slightly off-center.

Melanie and Adeline each loaded their 9mm Smith and Wesson shields, fired, and also hit slightly off-center. Not as great as Olivia, but very few people were.

With a push of the button, they pulled the targets up to twenty yards and repeated, ready, aim, fire. Line by line, mark by mark. As the targets got closer, Adeline's, Sunday's, and Melanie's accuracies increased, and Olivia's stayed on point. By the time they were pulling the targets down, the guys were nowhere to be seen.

Unloading their guns, they packed their remaining ammunition back in the boxes, and then headed back to the small holding room to grab their stuff.

"Olivia, why do you need to practice again?" Adeline asked.

"I don't want to get rusty."

"Says the natural-born gunslinger." Adeline popped her ass up onto a nearby counter.

"Hey, did you intimidate those men or something?" Max hollered from across the store.

"Blame Livi, it was her first bull's-eye at fifty yards that sent their pussy asses running." Adeline examined her nails as if she didn't have a care in the world. Olivia sneered. "Olivia, don't you have a thing for bearded guys?"

Olivia arched one brow, totally lost by Adeline's question.

"Think about it, Max is bearded, he's the only guy who can probably outshoot you, and he isn't intimidated by you.

Hell, he's the perfect man for you." Adeline winked at Olivia.

"Absolutely not." Olivia shook her head vehemently. "Not funny. He's old enough to be my dad, maybe my grandfather."

"I think Adeline is on to something. I mean, they'd be awesome together, and maybe we could get a discount on shit. You think?" Melanie gave a devious smile to Olivia.

"Stop, you guys are gross." Olivia flipped them off. "I hope you all get diarrhea while you are wearing white and there isn't a bathroom anywhere around . . . oh, and that you are surrounded by people."

"You love us, you know you do." Adeline kicked one foot out and lightly tapped Olivia. "It's just weird that Max deals with guns, and you're a fucking gunslinger. I can't help but think that it is a match made in heaven."

"I couldn't have thought up a better couple myself," Sunday added.

When Adeline sees Max coming over to join them, she changes the topic. Yes, they loved to pick on each other, but they rarely let other people in on the action. They'd never truly embarrass each other in front of others. "So, how's the business these days, Max?"

"The past few weeks have been driving me to drink, I tell ya. People are nuts, they come here for the wrong reasons, ya know?" Max ran his fingers along his mustache. "They come here when they are mad, thinking that firing a gun will help them let it out. They get pissed at me when I refuse to let them on my range. Then there are the ones who think they are all gangsta and know shit from watching television and movies. When they fill out the forms they mark, yes, to knowing how to handle a gun. This kind of shit is bad for business. If only we could give IQ tests along with background checks, but of course, that will never happen. They don't want anyone to feel forced into disclosing information that would make them uncomfortable, but then they wonder why we don't have all the information when the guy goes nuts and shoots people. They never understand that it is called selective enforcement. A slippery damn slope."

"Stay true, Max. You keep making people spend a day with you on the range before they buy their first gun, do things your way. We will always support you." Adeline patted his shoulder before picking up her duffle bag and heading out the door.

Chapter Nineteen

ADELINE

$\mathcal{I}$ t was Adeline's turn to cook and the truth was, she just didn't feel like it, so she picked up a pizza from Giordano's on her way home instead. She knew the girls would be on high alert immediately, since Adeline loved to cook, but her heart just wasn't in it. Her heart was firmly with a gorgeous man and his German Shepherd. Adeline wondered what they were doing right then as she grabbed a slice, poured herself a glass of vodka on ice, and dropped a slice of lime into it. Instead of heading into the living room, which was normally where they all ate and drank, she headed outside to the pool.

She needed to talk with the girls, they were best friends after all, would they criticize her for having feelings toward a client, or would they encourage her? Wait, was Riley even a client anymore? Swishing her legs back and forth, Adeline watched the swirls break into waves and then dissipate . . . oh the irony . . . love was much the same way. It was all swirls and then it hit waves and dissipated into nothingness.

"Boo." Adeline jumped at the sound of Melanie's voice as

she copped a squat next to her. "You were a million miles away, you didn't even move when I came out."

"I'm sorry, just got a lot on my mind."

"A lot on your mind or a hottie on your mind?" Melanie shoulder bumped her friend, obviously trying to get a smile out of her.

"It's that obvious, huh? I feel guilty. He's a client, or rather, was, right? I shouldn't be interested in him. I don't know, I can't explain it. He makes me feel something, something that I can't remember ever feeling before. But I'm scared." Adeline kicked her feet harder, splashing water.

"What are you scared of?"

"You."

Hurt crossed over Melanie's face at that confession.

"Sunday, Olivia."

"Whoa, what about us? Since when is the great Adeline Morgan scared of anyone?"

"I don't want to let you all down, I don't want to let myself down. I know the rules. We made them for a reason, professionalism. But . . ."

Melanie nodded. "Yeah, I see what you mean. It's risky. I don't think that you should take a chance. What if he's just like all the other guys and turns out to be scum?"

Adeline sniffled. "Yeah, that."

"Then again, what if he turns out to be one of the good guys? Someone who truly can fall in love with just one person for the rest of his life?"

Adeline kicked her feet again. "No such thing."

"Ad, even you know that's a broad brushstroke. Come on, you can't seriously think that, right?"

"No, I don't. But come on, it's unreasonable for me to like him this much when we haven't even really kissed."

"So, there have been some fake kisses?"

"Stop being stupid."

"Me? Do you hear yourself?"

"All I mean is that he has given me a little peck, but nothing heavy duty."

Melanie shrugged, "Uh-huh. And isn't that how all relationships start? Well, the ones that last anyway. Call me crazy, but you see there's this thing that has been going on for centuries and it's called love at first sight. Crazy, I know. But believe it or not, some people's souls or hearts or whatever it is just recognize each other. Maybe you two have that?"

"It isn't hearts or souls or whatever. It's pheromones. Science, Melanie, it's a real thing. My rational arguments aside, what about our rules, or Sunday and Olivia?"

"What fucking rule? I don't remember us ever having a rule that said you couldn't fall in love or even have a life."

"No, the one about mixing business with pleasure."

Melanie let out a loud laugh. "You idiot. That rule was made when we were all much younger and wilder. If you remember, back then it was way more likely that one of us might sleep with a relative of a client. Hell, between the four of us, our conquests totally topped seven-ways to Kevin Bacon. It was more like three ways to our house."

Adeline cracked up because it was sort of true.

"And as far as Sunday and Olivia go? They want what I want, and that is for you to be happy. We see some shitty things, but that doesn't mean that all men are Satan. If you think he will make you happy, then you owe it to him and yourself to find out. We've done our job for Loren, and now it is just dotting our i's and crossing our t's. Go see if he feels the way you do."

"But what if he doesn't?"

"Oh, but what if he does?"

≈

ADELINE'S HEART was beating a million miles a minute as she stood in front of Riley's door.

Hell, she had been standing there for five minutes and had halfway talked herself out of this crazy notion, but then her phone rang.

Swiping to answer and pressing his doorbell at the same time caused an explosion of noise. Well, it sounded more like an explosion because Adeline could hear Gerda barking from inside the house and through the phone.

"Adeline, I'm sorry. Can you hold on? Someone is at my door. *Platz*, Gerda." Riley gave the German command for Gerda to freeze, and silence fell in time for Adeline to hear the twisting of a lock. The door swung open, revealing the most gorgeous man she'd ever seen.

She took one step forward and Riley swept her into his arms. His mouth came down to meet hers and he gave her the kiss she'd been fantasizing about. His mouth was unrelenting as his tongue tangled with hers and his hands slid down either side of her waist and around her butt.

When he spun, he took her with him and then kicked the door closed, shutting them away from the rest of the world. She hadn't changed out of her work clothes from earlier, and for the first time, she was really glad that she was wearing a skirt. Riley worked his agile fingers down, down, until he was at the hem, and then deftly worked his way back up, his fingers sliding along her smooth legs as he bunched her skirt and lifted. Every inch of the way his hands deftly massaged her thighs until he could feel the heat radiating from her core. As he neared her center the heat intensified until her skirt was totally out of the way and he'd exposed her drenched, panty-clad pussy for his perusal.

"Let's take this into the bedroom." His voice was deep, deeper than Adeline had ever heard, but she followed him. Fuck who was she kidding, if he said to drink the red Kool-

Aid, she'd drink the fucking red Kool-Aid, so long as she got the fucking orgasm that he was building inside her.

They moved through his house, Riley walking behind her, his arms wrapped around as he used his body to guide her. The whole time his fingers were working at the buttons of her shirt, then the zipper on her skirt, and finally the clasp of her bra, which got dropped at the side of his bed a second before he was bending her forward over his comforter.

"I've dreamed of you, right here in this spot." His fingers danced down the length of her spine. His palms slid over her hips and her ass, smoothing their way over her curves as he slid her panties down her legs.

Adeline heard the sound of a buckle followed by a zipper, and the swish as his pants hit the floor. Then his mouth was on her skin, kissing along the path his hands had taken until he reached the curve of her shoulder.

When he slid his left hand between her legs, Adeline could feel her own moisture soaking him.

"God. Fuck, I love this. I fucking love the way my fingers sink into you."

When he stopped, Adeline almost lost it and a smart-ass retort popped into her mind as she tried to demand that he keep going, but he was flipping her over, looking down at her as if she was the most beautiful thing he'd ever seen. For looks like that, Adeline would keep her smart comments to herself.

"God, you're so smooth. I need to taste you. Lay back." Adeline did as ordered, her feet dangling off the bed. "I'm impressed, I thought it would take much more to get you to do as instructed."

Adeline pushed up to get off the bed but Riley was faster.

"Uh huh, you're here, exactly where I've wanted you for some time. Let me show you why it's okay to give in every now and then." Riley slid his hands under her ass and squeezed before removing her panties. Kneeling on the side of the bed like a man about to pray he came up between her legs, a calf resting on each shoulder, he lifted and leaned forward to breathe her in. He inhaled the mixture of musk and citrus as he used one hand to separate her folds. Lowering his head, he licked.

The gasp of breath that escaped Adeline only fueled Riley on as he increased his tempo, faster strokes, longer swipes. With his free hand, he moved it and slid one finger inside of her, then a second. His body was in perfect sync, tongue and fingers moved together in pace and so did his hips. He couldn't help it, but he was so fucking aroused just watching Adeline lose control that out of some primal reaction, his body was thrusting to the same beat.

Adeline bucked, her hips rising off the bed, but Riley used his forehead to press down and licked again. Up and down, side to side, she thrust, and he used his tongue and mouth to nibble and suck on her clit.

Chapter Twenty

RILEY

When her legs got heavier and a heat started radiating from her, he could tell that she was close. He curled his fingers into the *come here* gesture until she let out a low, drawn-out moan of pleasure.

"Riley, god . . . that—" A sharp gasp cut off her words, but he wasn't done yet. Not even close, so he took her right to the edge and backed her away, only to bring her right back up again.

When he couldn't stand the thought of not being inside her for one more second, he pulled back, stripped, and grabbed a condom from his dresser. All the while, Adeline panted and shifted, silently inviting him to take what she was so very clearly offering.

When he climbed back on top of her, he slid his arms under her—one moving up to press between her shoulder blades and the other snaking around her lower back—and rolled so she was straddling him. She was the most gorgeous woman he'd ever seen, and he wanted to watch her taking his cock. He wanted to see himself be buried deep inside her.

The expression on her face when she sank down onto him

was captivating, half-devious, half-lust drunk. And when she rocked her hips forward in a slow roll, Riley grabbed them, needing something to hold on to just as much as he needed to slow her. It was too fucking much.

Her head was thrown back, the column of her neck exposed, breasts on full display.

She was too much, too perfect in every way.

With the control of a saint, Riley slowly lifted her, completely enthralled by the way his body looked disappearing into her.

"Faster," she panted, and he gave her what she wanted.

Faster and deeper and harder until they were both lost to the sensations.

When her body fisted around him and he could feel her orgasm starting to vibrate through his own damn body, he rocked her clit against his own skin . . . and smiled.

"Oh, fuck," she cried breathlessly.

"Yep, that's exactly what I'm doing." Riley brought Adeline's mouth to his, taking it as thoroughly as he was taking her body.

He wanted to hear her shout his name.

He wanted to see that moment of ecstasy as it crossed her face.

He needed it more than he needed the heart in his damn chest.

"That's it, baby, let me see you come again."

Forward, up, down, and again. Adeline threw her head back as her body tensed and the heat rolled through her. Riley flipped her onto her back, threw one leg over his shoulder, and fucked her through her orgasm before chasing his own.

Chapter Twenty-One

ADELINE

*A*deline was fixing a pot of coffee when the elevator doors opened and Loren walked out, followed by Riley. She rocked on her heels, a little unsteady at the sight of him, since she's been avoiding his calls ever since their night together. Now here he was in their office, and he was gorgeous.

Guiding them in, Melanie and Olivia moved into the boardroom and took their normal seats, but this time Riley didn't sit next to Loren, instead he moved to the vacant seat on Adeline's right. She jumped when he placed a hand onto her leg.

"You look beautiful this morning, I've missed talking to you." He moved one hand to the nape of her neck, but Adeline flinched and pulled away.

"Yeah, been busy." She swallowed hard, trying not to face him.

Once everyone was settled Melanie began. "Loren, you realize that your husband hasn't been playing golf, correct?"

"Yeah, I sort of put those pieces together when he never mentioned his clubs were missing."

"Well, we know you need solid evidence for the prenuptial agreement, and we were able to get substantial proof to back this claim up." Sunday moved her mouse and brought up several photos, scrolling through in a slow still-life movie.

"Huh, that's Hillary Chatham. She's married."

"So is your husband," Adeline added.

"Did you or Greg know Hillary before she married Dan?" Sunday asked as she moved her mouse, looking for the next set of photos.

"No, why?"

Sunday brought up the yearbook photos from Stetson University and then they walked through what they knew about Tertiary Development and how Hillary and Greg owned the company together. Loren's complexion grew sallow when Sunday told her about the land that she had for Noelle and how Greg had forged her name. He'd filed a quit claim deed and sold it to Tertiary with the sole intention of having Tertiary, his own company, sell it to the city for a fuck-ton amount of profit. Loren threw one hand to her mouth as if she was trying not to vomit.

"Are you okay, Loren? If you want to stop here, we can. We can bring in our attorney and let him handle everything from this point on if you'd like." Adeline reached forward and clasped Loren's hands.

"No, I want to get that son of a bitch. It's one thing to screw me over, but his daughter? How dare he. She's only four years old. She's innocent, and he wants to steal from her? Oh hell no. What else do you have? Let's fry him."

Adeline clapped her hands together. Their clients were usually divided fifty-fifty at this point. Some got mad and some got depressed. Adeline always had more fun with those that got pissed.

"How do I get my land back?"

"That's easy, it's yours. Since inheritance isn't considered marital property, Greg didn't have the authority to sell it. That means, Tertiary bought stolen property, and they are out any money they paid plus whatever damages you would like to go after them for."

"What about the deal with the city?"

"He will have to handle that, it's considered a major conflict of interest to have the city purchase from your own business, especially on a land deal such as this. This particular deal will require some serious investigations, and they will probably bring in an interim mayor during that time," Melanie explained.

Sunday clicked a few more pictures and then turned on the audio from the luncheon at Cooper's Hawk.

"And who is she? I thought that Hillary was the owner of Tertiary."

"Keep listening," Sunday warned.

And Loren did as Sunday instructed and slowly it all made sense. "So how many women is he screwing?"

"We only have been able to find those two, but we don't think they know about each other. We think they each believe that he's leaving you for them," Adeline explained.

"Good riddance to bad rubbish, they can have him. Not that they'll be able to keep him happy—hell, I don't think the entire squad of Dallas Cowboys cheerleaders could keep him happy, not as long as he thinks someone might have had them first. So, what's next?" Loren was practically bouncing in her seat. Revenge looked good on her.

"Now, if Riley is willing, we have him call and see if he can get Trinity's contact information, explain that he has some questions for her, perhaps about selling his land parcel to the city or about selling it at a loss once it is rezoned. Let's see if Greg gives over the contact information or if he insists on meeting with them. Then, Loren, you call Hillary and invite her to lunch, be concerned about her sudden onset of migraine headaches."

"Where do we want to meet them?" Riley asked, seemingly totally onboard with this idea.

"For something like this, we have a pub that we like to use, it's called Sixes. It generally doesn't open until four, but the owner Vivian opens it for us if the need arises. You can regale Greg with stories about how you know the owner so you asked her to open early just for you guys."

Riley nodded and then pulled out his phone.

Everyone sat with bated breath trying to figure out what was being said on the other end of the line, until the last sentence, then they knew that Greg was all in.

"Perfect, Adeline and I will see you and Trinity at noon for lunch at Sixes. Do you need the address?"

Melanie quickly jotted down it down and passed it in front of Riley.

"Yeah, it's off Church Street." He disconnected and smiled. "He's in, but he wouldn't give me her info. He said that he wanted to make sure that I was treated fairly." Riley closed his phone and put it away, the whole time keeping one hand on Adeline's thigh.

"What bullshit," Loren mumbled and then pulled out her phone to call Hillary and set up their lunch.

RILEY AND ADELINE walked into Sixes at eleven thirty and were greeted by a woman with wide eyes and coal-black hair. "Vivian." Adeline's smile was warm and easy. "Thank you so much for doing this. This is Riley, his sister is the one with the asshole."

"You know that I'd do anything for you four," Vivian said

before turning to Riley. "It's nice to meet you. It's always good to see family supporting one another."

"Are we all set up?" Adeline glanced to the employee's-only door as she spoke, and Vivian nodded.

"Yeah. Piper is already in the backroom, and she will stay back there unless needed."

I turned to Riley and explained. "We hire an off-duty deputy or police officer for the confrontation time as an extra safety measure."

"I have several staff members here today," Vivian added. "It was unavoidable since today is truck day and I'm not inventorying all that product by myself."

"Is Duck in back too?"

"That man is here before I am most days. I'll tell him you said hi. For now, though, you two can have a seat over by the windows so you can see them walking in, okay?"

"Got it. Thanks, Viv."

Vivian disappeared into the kitchen and Adeline and Riley settled in to wait.

"Show time," Adeline said as Greg's car pulled into the parking lot. Sunday must have relayed the warning, because Mikki, their server for the day, and Danny, the bartender, both took their places in the dining area.

When Greg and Trinity walked in, Riley stood and greeted them and then waited for them to take their seats before reclaiming his own. The four of them had just placed their drink order when on cue the plan went into full operation.

Adeline's phone started ringing. "Excuse me, I'm so sorry, I thought I had silenced that." Adeline grabbed her phone and then pretended to look contrite when she answered. "Hi, Loren?"

"Adeline, I was just calling to see if you were available for lunch."

"Ohh. I wish I could, but actually I'm with Riley and your husband. We're having lunch at Sixes. He and Riley are talking about the land, remember? The realtor is here as well."

"Adeline, Loren does not get involved in my mayoral business. Please stop," Greg's voice was curt.

"Oh, I'm sorry. It's just that Loren was the one who's been encouraging Riley to do this with you and the realtor, so she already knew. I didn't think. I'm sorry."

"Riley, perhaps we should meet another time when you can meet alone and in a more professional setting." Greg stood.

"Loren, I better go." Adeline hung up but right then Mikki came over and delivered the drinks. "Here you go, and the appetizers you ordered will be up momentarily." Mikki directed her eyes toward Vivian.

Awesome, Vivian was trying to help keep him here. Adeline just hoped that Riley wouldn't ask, *what appetizers?* But he was smarter than that. Instead, he played a different card. "Greg, I totally understand, in fact I think I understand more than you are saying."

Greg looked at the both of them with a bored expression.

"You aren't really interested in doing business, you are just trying to appease me for Loren's sake. I had a suspicion when you were over an hour late for our first meeting, but I wasn't sure until we had dinner at the Bohemian and there wasn't much mentioned about the project, just a lot of boasting that I was your brother-in-law, as if you were trying to solidify that we couldn't do business together. And now this? Loren is involved a lot—hell, you have her run most of your fundraiser dinners. You're willing to leave over Adeline talking to your wife, my sister, and discussing something that she already knows about? Fine. I'll still make my donation, but I can donate it to the county instead of the city."

"Riley, no, that isn't it."

Adeline reached over and squeezed Riley's hand under the table. His speech had worked, and Greg was trying to backpedal. "Maybe I was a bit hasty."

Adeline, being the bitch she sometimes prided herself on being, decided to shove that proverbial knife a little deeper. "Once again, Greg, I'm sorry. I know that you don't think very highly of me, but your wife was inviting me to join her, she and her friend from the other night were going to lunch and I think it was nice of her to think of me."

"What friend from the other night?" Greg asked, shifting just the smallest amount.

"The one who she wanted me to meet, but I didn't get to because the woman was sick with a headache."

White . . . no ashen. Yes, ashen, that was the perfect descriptive word for Greg's complexion. He was ashen. But Adeline didn't get to see if there was a more putrid color than ashen because the door to Sixes opened and in walked Loren and Hillary Chatham.

"I'm sorry to interrupt, I just felt so bad for Greg getting furious with you," Loren announced as she moved toward their table.

"Loren, this is a private business luncheon. You and Adeline can catch up another time."

Loren, to her credit, ignored him and turned to Trinity. "Oh, I'm sorry, I don't think we've had a chance to meet. I'm Loren, Greg's wife."

"I'm Trinity Reynolds." The woman moved to shake Loren's hand, but Hillary had finally had enough.

"Excuse me, you're who?" Hillary asked, her voice at a breaking point.

"I'm Trinity Reynolds." The fake Trinity reached into her purse and pulled out a business card—a real business card—for Tertiary Development.

"Hillary." Greg's voice was cold as ice. "You need to calm down."

"No, no I don't. I need to know what the hell is going on because I know for a fact that this bottle-blonde is *not* Trinity Reynolds, nor is she a part of Tertiary Development."

Loren took a step back, a wide smile crossing her face. Adeline stayed in place so her pendant could catch everything on camera.

"Maybe you both should have a seat." Riley stood and pulled out a chair for his sister to sit.

"No, they were just leaving." Greg once again tried to get his wife to leave, but the woman just kept that triumphant smile on her lips.

"No, Greg, you don't give orders here. I don't think you get the full picture, none of you do." Loren's voice was calm and cool. "You see, I know who you are, Heather"—Loren looked at the Trinity impersonator before pinning her gaze on the woman she walked in with—"and Hillary, aka Trinity, aka Tertiary, aka fellow Stetson alumnus. And, Greg, I know all about your affairs with both women."

"His what?" Both women shouted in unison. "You are sleeping with her?" They each pointed to the other.

"Shut up, both of you. Are you shocked that he cheated on you or lied to you? Hello, he's married to me and has been lying to me and cheating on me. When will all of the dumbass women of the world learn? If a man's willing to cheat *for* you, then he is also willing to cheat *on* you." Loren gave Adeline a disbelieving look.

"I have no clue why everyone's so upset, you all should be high-fiving each other because I think that if there are three or more it qualifies as a team. Yeah, you got yourselves a team of Greg's women." Adeline pointed to Hillary and to Heather and then wrapped an arm around Loren to let her know that she wasn't really intending anything mean to her. She couldn't get over the stupidity of her own sex, it really was heart-breaking to see how these two skanks thought that they were the only woman Greg was having an affair with.

"As I was saying." Loren's voice was a bit louder. "I also know about your and Hillary's attempt to steal Noelle's trust and your and Heather's"—Loren directed this to Greg—"plan to purchase Riley's property for dirt cheap and then resell it to the city for a large amount, only this time you were planning to cut Hillary out." As if remembering the other woman was standing next to her, Loren turned to Hillary. "Tell me, does your husband know you've been sleeping with Greg?"

"What do you want?" Greg still was acting superior.

"I need all three of your driver's licenses so that I can make a copy."

"I'm not giving you mine," Heather pulled her purse close.

"Fine." Loren opened her purse, pulled out her iPad, and then pressed play. It was their conversation at the table at Cooper's Hawk and their sex-capade in the car.

"That's illegal, you can't use that against me. You broke the law, you're just as much in the wrong." Greg pointed at the iPad.

"Come on, now, Greg, you went to law school. You should know that discussions that take place in public aren't considered confidential. I don't know for sure, but I would bet money that having sex in public falls into the same category. In public, we accept the assumed belief that someone is going to see us or overhear us. That is why street cameras and cameras inside stores and restaurants are legal. You carried this on in public. So do as Loren asked."

All three people handed over their driver's license, which was a sigh of relief since they hadn't been able to learn anything else about Heather and had no clue of her last name. Adeline held each ID up to her pendant and waited until Sunday gave the go ahead before handing it back.

"You." Greg pointed at Adeline. "Your necklace is a camera. You're the one who has turned Loren into a mouthy . . . I should have known. I told Riley you weren't the kind to keep around."

"Yes, I know. Remember? I overheard you? But as you can tell, I don't value your opinion or"—Adeline leaned forward and looked at Hillary and then Heather—"your taste in women."

Riley stood, his fists clenched.

Adeline realized that this had just escalated and that they needed Piper before it got out of hand. Shit. She reached for her purse and grabbed her stun gun just in case, although truthfully, she'd like to unclip her gun, but you can't win them all.

"If I hear you say one more derogatory comment about her, you'll be eating your food through a straw." Riley's nostrils were flared.

Adeline tugged on his hand to get him to sit and then pointed toward the hallway, where Piper stood in full uniform. All heads turned to where Adeline had directed her gaze.

"You brought the fucking cops?" Greg was no longer the cool or controlled picture of a professional politician.

"It's a security measure. She was hired by me just in case this got out of hand. Now, if you'll let Loren finish and then we can all get back to our regularly scheduled programs."

Adeline met Heather's eyes and found that the woman was smirking. The bitch thought this whole thing was funny. What the hell? Then, spying a small movement of her arm, Adeline scooted her chair back and tried to follow the movement of Heather's hand without being too obvious. The woman was unrelenting, she was headed for Greg's crotch, and believe it or not, he was pushing her hand away.

That was the final straw, the breaking point for Adeline,

having had it with the twenty-two-year-old bimbo. "Heather, you might want to keep your hands to yourself, you're in a lot of trouble. Oh . . . and close your legs . . . Greg's breath totally stinks." She had said it without thinking, and Riley froze for just a second before he started laughing so hard his eyes watered. Yep, sometimes even she was shocked by what came out of her own mouth.

Loren was also at her breaking point. "I'd suggest that you all wait to hear from my attorney. Greg, you might want to find somewhere else to stay."

"That's my home."

"And that was your daughter's trust you and your married girlfriend tried to steal and sell to a city that trusted you enough to put you in office. The locks and alarm code have already been changed. If you set foot on the property, I will have you removed."

Loren stood and strode out of Sixes. Adeline and Riley waited for her to leave.

"She just left me." Hillary was shocked.

Adeline shook her head. "Maybe you can hitch a ride with Greg and Heather, they came together."

"All right, folks, we're closing up," Vivian announced. "You all have caused quite a stir." Piper still didn't say a word as she moved to the door and held it open for Greg, Heather, and Hillary walked out.

"Thanks, Piper. Vivian, this is for you and your staff." Adeline handed her an envelope. "Piper, this is for you."

"You know that I can't take tips. You pay directly to the county and they pay me."

"Yep, I know, not a tip. It's some stuff from Max's. It's a gift as friends."

"Thanks. Nice seeing you again, Riley." Piper waved as Adeline and Riley headed out.

Chapter Twenty-Two

ADELINE

She didn't want to miss today, because today was the day they were turning Loren's case over to Barrett Huxley, attorney extraordinaire. So, when she walked into the office two minutes early, she was damn proud of herself.

"Good morning." Adeline waved.

"Morning. Grab your coffee, Loren should be here soon." Adeline watched as Melanie picked up a stack of papers and headed toward the boardroom, and then she followed.

When Loren arrived, there were circles under her eyes and she didn't appear quite as put together as she normally did. "Can I fix you some coffee, Loren?"

Adeline was already up and moving, prepared to get the woman a drink whether she wanted one or not, when Loren answered. "Yes, please. Cream and sugar."

"Are you okay?" Melanie asked, leaning forward a bit, as if her concern was forcing her closer to the woman in a silent show of support. "Has Greg been bothering you?"

"He's worried that I'm going to go to the press. He's only harassing me to know what I'm going to do. He's trying to get me to wait until after the election. As if he doesn't have bigger things to worry about—like jail. But I'm not going to wait. I want this done with now, I've wasted too much time on him. I need to be free, my daughter and I need to move on."

"Then what is it?"

"You're going to think this sounds stupid because all of you are so strong and confident." Adeline wanted to laugh, because secretly inside sometimes she felt like a scared little girl trying to play dress up. "When you think you've found the one, you believe that it's going to be forever. You think that he's different from all the rest. You ask yourself how you got so lucky." Loren took a sip of her coffee then stared out the window overlooking downtown Orlando. "But you wake up one day and find out that he wasn't different at all, you were just blind. You feel like the world's biggest fool. Somehow, when this all comes out, Greg will pull through it."

"Shit always rises," Adeline hissed.

"But me? I'll be the one they all feel sorry for. The one who couldn't keep her husband satisfied, the one who was too stupid to realize he was having affairs. And Noelle? What about my baby? Greg will move on, make another family. He doesn't know how to balance. Noelle and I will be the old family and he will never see her again. My daughter won't know what it's like to have a father-daughter dance at her wedding, or to have her dad scare away her dates."

Adeline bit her tongue, refusing to point out the obvious, which was that Noelle probably wouldn't have had any of those things with Greg anyway. The comment was just her way of lashing out against the nails Loren was driving into the coffin containing Adeline and Riley's relationship. A way to hide the brutal blows she was feeling and the realization that there was no way Adeline would ever end up in Loren's position. She wouldn't allow it. She was way too smart to allow some man to control her or her world. No way. Adeline strummed her nails along the edge of the table, the tap-tap-tap might as well have been a hammer, because each sound was knocking sense back into her. She'd almost let her guard down with Riley, almost. But, the fates were looking after her. Just when she started to cave, shit like this would pop up, a constant reminder that the only person a woman could count on was herself.

Melanie spoke low. "Loren, you didn't have those things either, and you turned out fine."

"I had Riley. Noelle doesn't have an older brother."

Olivia stepped in, saying, "Noelle doesn't have a brother yet, but there's still plenty of time. You may find the perfect man and get remarried and give her a brother or sister. Who knows, maybe the guy will be a single dad and have a son who is older than Noelle. What if the dad loves Noelle like she is his own and the son sees her as the sister he never had? You can't close the lid yet. You're so young. We have a file of clients who will tell you that the second time around is the best. They're so much wiser. They know what to look for but more than that, they know their own worth."

"You think so?" Loren wiped her face.

"Know so," Olivia assured her.

Adeline, who couldn't seem to form any words that were reassuring, pulled out a piece of paper and slid it to Melanie.

The Iron Ladies had always found that keeping newly single women involved and busy was the number one way to keep their clients from falling back into bad habits or broken relationships.

For Loren, they suggested she move and start fresh with Noelle, somewhere that had more children. They also found the names of a few playgroups that had several single dads in the group. Always nice to know that there are options.

At just before eleven, Adeline excused herself and went to wait for Barrett in the parking lot. As usual, the man was early, and as she was walking out, he was walking in, so she turned right back around and led him upstairs. What she really wanted to do was walk outside, get into her car, and go find a deserted stretch of road to open up on.

"Loren, I'd like you to meet Barrett Huxley, he's who will be handling the legal aspects of your case. We absolutely trust him with everything. He is the best. Barrett, this is your newest client, Loren."

"We're going to leave the two of you alone. Barrett, let us know if you need anything, and when you decide that you want a meeting with both parties so that we can help wrap things up on our end, let me know."

"Will do, Mel."

Melanie stood, the others followed suit. "Adeline, you don't look like you feel good, we don't have anything today, why don't you go home and rest."

Adeline moved to her chair and picked up her bag and keys. Melanie was right. She needed to go home and rest. No, she needed to call Riley. No, she needed to figure out what in the hell she was doing.

Sliding behind the wheel of her V8, Adeline rolled down all the windows. She turned up the radio to some old-school Billy Idol and hit the on ramp to I-4. She wasn't sure where she was going, she just needed the freedom and the open road to clear her mind.

She drove for an hour before turning into her own driveway. Unfortunately, the ride hadn't helped clear her mind one bit. She was still just as confused.

Walking into her bedroom, she pulled out her phone and sent a text to Riley.

ADELINE: Can we talk?

Riley: Want me to call now?

Adeline: Busy right now. Free tonight? Dinner?
Riley: Want to meet at Lakeside?
Adeline: Sure. Seven?
Riley: I'll make reservations. See you then.

ADELINE POWERED off her phone before curling under the covers and falling asleep. She didn't wake until a little after five and had to rush to get ready and meet Riley over at Lakeside. If anyone had asked her, she would have told them that today had been a major clusterfuck. Adeline tried to live by a schedule, but she couldn't be on time to save her life. No matter what she did today, she felt as if she was running behind.

At five minutes after seven, she was running down the plank-wood walkway, under mason jars that held electric votive lights, toward the front door of the restaurant.

Riley was standing next to the hostess stand and smiled when she walked in. When he wrapped an arm around her, Adeline stiffened.

"Sorry I'm late."

"It's okay." Riley placed a soft kiss on Adeline's temple before they fell into step behind the hostess as she led them to their table.

She had no idea what she was going to say to him, but she did know that Loren's words had resonated with her. She was destined for heartbreak, and Riley was just the type of guy who could do it. In fact, he wouldn't just break her heart. He'd shatter it into a million pieces.

It wasn't a risk she was willing to take.

She'd allowed herself to feel broken once before, and she'd ended up in rehab. Not again, never again. She wasn't going down that fucking rabbit hole.

Taking a deep breath, then a drink of water, followed by another deep breath, she set her menu down. "Riley."

"What is on your mind Addy?"

There it was, that first crack in her heart, when he called her Addy . . .

Chapter Twenty-Three

RILEY

*R*iley sat quiet, only half-listening to Adeline's jumbled attempt at explaining why they would not work. From the moment he saw her arrive in the lobby, he knew something was coming. She had played this game before, pulling back just as they were starting to get close. He kept telling himself to tread carefully, sometimes with Adeline it was like early spring and walking across your lawn at the crack of dawn. Little ice crystals coated each blade of grass but with each step they cracked, giving way to the still-dormant life below.

Riley gripped his napkin, he had to do something with his hands or he was likely to stand up and start breaking shit, starting with the neck of the beautiful woman sitting across from him. She wouldn't even look at him. Fuck.

It didn't take Sherlock Holmes to see the fear that was masking her true feelings. He had felt something for her that very first moment he'd laid eyes on her. She drove him crazy and ignited a fire in him. Her involuntary responses, like the sigh she let out when he'd touched her, and the goosebumps that peppered her skin when their eyes locked, told him she felt it too.

But dammit, if only she'd open up and tell him how she'd been hurt, instead of wearing her injuries like a prized coat, out there for all to admire. If she needed time, he could give it, as long as she didn't ask for space apart.

If they were apart then he'd never be able to build her trust and get her to open up. But here he was staring at the woman who did chaotic things to him, she stalked his thoughts, just watching the indecision and uncertainty swim in her features drove him crazy.

Adeline accepted a fresh glass of water from the waiter and sat it on the table before her, tracing the pads of her thumbs across the thick condensation on the glass, her eyes examining the tablecloth before her.

The waiter paused a moment, "Are you ready to order?" But Adeline didn't meet the waiter's eyes, so Riley waited. The young man took his exit upon feeling the overwhelming tension permeating the air.

"I want to tell you something? Will you listen?"

Adeline nodded, maintaining her fascination with her water glass. Riley watched her carefully knowing full-well she wanted to run; one false step and she would bolt.

"I know that you're scared about something and I have no problem slowing us"—Riley gestured first to himself then to Adeline—"down. I'm not going anywhere. If you just want to take more time to sort through whatever you have going on up there," Riley tapped his temple, "then I'm fine with that. We will slow down."

"I don't need more time to know for certain." Her eyes returned to Riley for just a moment before darting back to her glass, the finality of her words piercing his heart. Riley's jaw tightened as he felt the need to lash out. His hands dropped to his lap and he balled up his fists.

"We won't work. You're good, don't get me wrong, I'm just not ready to be monogamous. I don't know that I ever will be. You want too much from me."

Riley was taken aback by her words. *He wanted too much from her?* Was she on fucking drugs? Call him a freak, sure he wanted more than sex, but he wasn't expecting her to change who she was or give up her life.

"I just don't see us going anywhere beyond sex."

"You cold-hearted..." he mumbled.

"What, cold-hearted what Riley? Bitch? Really?"

"If you would just let me finish." Riley snapped and leaned back in his seat taking a few deep breaths, happy she had not let him finish his last thought. His movement caught the attention of a gentleman seated next to them; Riley glared back at him, silently persuading the man to return to his own fucking business. When the man finally got the hint, Riley returned his gaze to the infuriating woman across from him.

He searched the depths of her eyes, her expression, anything for a glimmer of hope that she was just confused, but he found none.

Riley sat forward and lightly gripped the table's edge, chiding himself to maintain control. "Adeline I feel sorry for you. You are a scared little girl that has never grown up and learned how to face her feelings."

Adeline broke her attention from the glass. "You know nothing about me. Besides, I can't do this with you. You're my client. It was a mistake. It was just sex. I'm sorry."

Fuck no she didn't. Riley fell back into his seat and hooked his hands beneath his armpits. "You don't mean that."

"Don't tell me what I mean."

"We're more than that, Adeline. There's more to us than just sex."

"You don't understand, Riley. There is no *us*."

Unable to take any more, Riley pushed his chair back and

stood. "I don't feel much like eating, after all. I'm assuming you're okay to get home the same way you got here?"

Adeline nodded and then placed her napkin on the top of the forgotten menu.

Riley took one final look into Adeline's steely blue eyes, which hadn't seemed so cold and calculating the last time he'd gazed into them. Tonight, however, they were unfeeling and uncaring. He gazed about the room, feeling the walls caving in on him. He had to get out of here; he had to breathe.

He felt like such a fucking fool.

That he'd actually considered using the word love with her blew his mind. Hell, he didn't think that he'd ever used it with a woman other than his family. He marched out to his truck and got in, but he didn't leave, not yet. Even as mad as he was, he still needed to make sure Adeline got into her car safely.

He was shocked that she sat at the table for several minutes after he left. At first, Riley's mind played tricks on him, telling him that she was waiting for another guy. But when none showed up and Adeline finally gathered her belongings, he could see her tear-streaked face.

She didn't bother trying to wipe them away as she got into her car, revved the engine, and drove off.

It was only after she was out of sight that Riley allowed the full force of what had just happened to hit him.

She'd fucking thrown them away, dismissed the feeling they'd shared and was able to walk away. Fuck. He really didn't know her at all.

Chapter Twenty-Four

ADELINE

*A*deline dressed in her power color—black. It had been two weeks since she'd seen Riley, and she was confident he would accompany his sister today. After all, today was the day Loren and Greg met with their attorneys. They decided to meet at Iron Ladies, or as the building directory listed them, Women's Counseling Center.

Lights were turned on in the small side offices and the boardroom was prepped. Not wanting to turn around when she heard the elevator ding, Adeline took a seat at the back of the boardroom. Melanie, Olivia, and Sunday would be in an office waiting to jump in if they were needed.

She knew he was there before she heard him. Her skin tingled, and her heart picked up speed. His aftershave, a mix of spices and fresh-cut grass, permeated the room. Adeline gipped her pen and continued writing in her notepad, forcing herself not to look up.

Chairs squeezed, leather crinkled, and a deep exhalation of breath seemed to be coming through a speaker. Adeline knew that was just her mind playing tricks on her.

Barrett was the first to speak. "Mr. Delaney should be here by now."

Adeline looked up and locked eyes with Riley, who was staring at her. His gaze was piercing.

"We'll give him about ten more minutes and then file with the court." Barrett tapped a pen against the mahogany table and only stopped when he wanted to jot down a few notes about whatever he was working on.

At nine thirty, Barrett started packing his stuff up. "I'll let the courts know that neither Mr. Delaney or his attorney were present."

Just then the elevator dinged and everyone turned. Out walked a laughing Greg with his attorney, like they had some inside joke.

"Mr. Delaney, council." Barrett's tone was clipped. "You are a half hour late for mediation, we just reported you as a no-show to the courts. I'm heading back to my office."

Greg's face lost its jovial appearance and his eyes cut to his lawyer. But the man next to him just glared at Barrett. Adeline was sure there was some kind of secret code between lawyers that said stuff like this should be overlooked, but she was also sure that Barrett didn't care.

"Mrs. Delaney, Mr. Huxley, sorry that we were late. It's my fault. I got caught in court. I had instructed my client to wait for me, so he's been downstairs."

Adeline stood. "Oh, the building and parking lot have total video surveillance that the tenants have access to. Let me go grab so we can verify really fast." Adeline took a step.

"Let's not waste any more time with that, I'm sure that Mr. Huxley is as busy as I am. We can sort that out later." Greg's attorney, who still hadn't introduced himself, set his briefcase onto the table.

"You two are late, and it isn't up to me whether this meeting continues. It's up to Loren and the court-approved mediator and mediation facility." Adeline was still standing and couldn't hold it back, she smirked.

Greg, obviously used to Loren being a pushover, plopped himself into a chair and sat. "This place operates on money and the good graces of the city, I'm sure that they will make time."

"Let's get it over with, he deserves to know what I'm asking for." Loren sat back down, with Riley at her side.

Adeline made her way back down to the end of the table.

"What is she doing in here in the first place?" Greg pointed at Adeline.

"She's a counselor, this is her office building, and I asked her to be here," Loren said, leaving no room for him to counter.

"As we mentioned, she's a court-approved mediator."

"I don't want her in here. We won't continue until she's gone."

Adeline shook her head, she'd seen the cocky bravado one too many times and oh how she loved seeing the asshole-ex deflate.

Barrett raised one brow and stared down Greg's attorney. "Care to explain to your client how this works, and then explain to him the ramifications of being late and lying about being here when we all know he wasn't downstairs for the last thirty minutes?" Adeline loved when Barrett's facetious side came out. "My client and the mediator are willing to let us continue, do we do that or not?"

Greg and his attorney exchanged looks before both nodded their agreement.

"We'd like to start with what Loren Delaney is seeking." Barrett flipped to the first page of the prepared documents.

"She gets nothing, we have a prenuptial agreement." Greg was a worthless asshat.

"Correct. Please let me continue. Here is what Mrs.

Delaney is seeking." Barrett passed a copy over to Greg and his attorney.

"I have a statement from our bank, there is not that much money in the account. Look, it is dated today." Greg tossed the slip over.

"I've included a bank slip as well as six months' worth of bank records in this file." Barrett slid a folder to each person, including Adeline. "I've attached a copy of your bank records that Loren got showing proof of the balance that day you all met at Sixes. If you look closely, you'll be able to see all the numbers."

Adeline didn't have to look that closely, nor did she want to. Barrett had stapled the bank receipt to two different items, a photo of Greg and Heather making out in the parking lot after their lunch with Riley and Adeline, and the forged quit claim deed.

Greg gripped both sides of the folder and tore it, then tore it again, tossing the shreds back at Barrett.

"Greg you need to stay calm." Barrett spoke like he was dealing with a toddler instead of a grown adult.

It was a tone he would use several times over the next two hours, because Greg continued to try to intimidate everyone in the room, not realizing that it wouldn't work. He needed to bow down gracefully and hope that Loren didn't go to the press. But he just didn't seem to be grasping that idea.

"Fine, my client will agree to Mrs. Delany's demands provided she turns over all copies of all photos and signs an affidavit stating that she will not discuss anything that happened in this room today. Same goes for her brother. The rest of you are already under a legal client confidentiality agreement.

"I will not sign anything nor will my brother." Adeline grinned, feeling proud of her protege. Loren wasn't giving him an inch. "Greg, you're going to do the right thing for once, simply because it is the right thing. All I'm asking for is half of our marital assets, which includes all the shit you thought you hid, and that you pay a fair amount of child support until Noelle is eighteen or out of college."

Greg scoffed.

Loren jumped out of her seat and pointed her finger toward his face. "I'm tired of your fucking attitude." Loren jerked at the realization that she'd said the F-word.

And, this time, Adeline couldn't hide it anymore, she let the grin show. She was so proud of this woman and the *she-balls, chick-dick, chesticles,* whatever the fuck it was nowadays, she'd grown.

"I don't know you. The Loren I married would have never said fuck."

"Well, the guy I married was going to be faithful and try not to steal from his daughter and scam the city. I think saying fuck is the lesser of those evils, don't you?"

Adeline sat at the end of the table nodding.

"As long as you do what is right, give me back my property free and clear, split our assets down the middle, and stay the hell out of my life, I won't file forgery charges, which, in case you forgot, is a felony of the third degree in this state. I won't share any of these photos, and I won't say a single thing. Neither will Riley. But the truth of the matter is you shouldn't be trusted to hold a public office. You shouldn't be anyone's dad, because you're scum. And all I want is for Noelle to forget that she has any of your blood in her and to once again enjoy being a little girl."

About halfway through Loren's rant, Greg turned a lovely shade of purple, and Adeline hoped that Sunday had enough forethought to snap a picture of it. Maybe they would frame it and hang it in their secured room as a trophy.

"I'll file the paperwork for Mrs. Delaney, and let's hope that you can have more control over your client and convince him of the intelligence of letting this be a non-contested divorce." Barrett stood and so did Greg and his attorney. Barrett waited for them to leave before turning to Loren. "I'll get the paperwork filed and have a copy couriered over to you. In the meantime, call if you need anything."

"Thank you, Mr. Huxley." Loren hugged him before Barrett left as well.

"Loren, you know what this is?" Adeline placed an orchid-colored plastic business card into Loren's hand. "It is not for you to keep but for you to pass on if you ever meet the right woman who truly needs us."

"Too bad you don't accept men, or I'd pass it to Dan Chatham." Everyone let out a groan at Loren's sick sense of humor, because they had no clue whether Dan was even aware of his wife's antics, and not a single one of them was inclined to tell him.

Chapter Twenty-Five

LOREN

*L*oren had rented a small home with a beautiful yard in Lake Nona, it wasn't too far from Riley. The owners had allowed her to move in as a rental while she was making arrangements to buy the place. Noelle had been used to her dad not being around, so the only change for her was a new preschool and a new bedroom.

As usual, Riley ate most of his meals at his sister's new home. "Are you going to call her?"

"Call who?" Riley looked up from the pasta primavera he'd been pushing around his plate.

"Really? You're going to treat me like I'm stupid too? Don't. Greg did that for enough years to last me a lifetime."

"I don't know what you want from me. It's been three weeks. She hasn't even bothered to text."

"And you've reached out to her?"

"You just don't get it. We were doing great. I thought that we'd finally crossed some invisible wall she had built, and then she shows up at the restaurant and something in her had changed. She was scared to death. Clearly, she doesn't trust me enough to talk to me about whatever it is. Hell, I don't think she even trusts herself to know why she was so scared." Riley got up and moved to the kitchen and started loading the dishwasher.

This had become part of their nightly routine, he'd wash while Loren went and gave Noelle her bath and then got her ready for bed. It was weird, but Loren loved this time, it was the first time she actually had help, even if it was from her brother.

When Loren came out, she turned off the television and sat at the table, waiting for Riley to sit. They needed to talk this out. She hated seeing what he was going through, and after all her brother had done for her, if she could help him then she would.

"Talk to me, Ri. Just because my marriage didn't work out, it doesn't mean I don't understand love, I do."

"I know you do. But don't. It was sex, that's all it was."

"Riley Christopher Thomas, how dare you. That is probably the most crude thing you've ever said to me. How would you feel if someone said they were only using me for sex?"

Riley threw his hands over his ears, trying to muffle her words.

"Or what if someone said that about Noelle when she got older?"

Riley cringed. "I'd kill them."

"Then why would you say something like that about Adeline? There are people who love her like you love us." Loren looked at her brother, letting her disappointment show.

"No, not me. Her. Adeline was only in it for sex. She wasn't in it for anything more. I was the one who had fallen. Not her. I should have known, she sees so much heartbreak every day in her career that it was bound to break her." Riley dried his hands and then started the dishwasher. "Love you, but I'm all talked out. I'm headed home."

Loren watched her brother walk out of her house and down the sidewalk toward his own house. She knew she owed it to the two people she believed had helped her more than anyone else. Riley was wrong, Adeline was in love with him, she saw it every time Adeline looked at him. There was just something about a woman who was in love, her eyes sparkled and she radiated with her emotions. That was how she saw Adeline every time Riley was near.

Reaching for her cell phone, Loren called the only other person she could think of who had a vested interest in seeing Adeline happy . . . Melanie. She'd only called her once before, and that had been the first time she'd called the Iron Ladies asking for help.

"Hello?"

"Hi, Melanie, this is Loren. Don't let anyone know that you're talking to me. But do you have time to talk?"

"Sure. Hold on a second." Loren listened to the tinkling sound of keys, the open and close of a door, and then the open and slam of what could only be a car door. "Okay, I'm in my car. It's the only place I know they won't listen in."

Loren let out a laugh. She'd never lived in a dorm or a sorority house, but imagined living with three other women had to be difficult. "Well, the thing is, I know someone who needs your help—or rather, the help of the Iron Ladies."

"So soon? Usually our clients don't pass the card on for months or even years." Melanie was genuinely surprised. "If you gave them the card, then have them call us and set up an appointment. We really need to speak to them directly. We find it's best that you distance yourself as much as possible from the situation."

Loren let Melanie finish explaining how to handle an obviously common issue they faced before continuing. "It isn't that easy or that kind of problem. It's sort of a different type of case. I know that you only work with women but—"

"Loren, we were all goofing off the other day about Dan, but the truth is, we don't accept men as clients. We don't feel trained for the situation, there is so much more involved than just getting the dirt, as you know. We want to make sure you get your confidence back and you are stable and can face the world as the woman you once were, only wiser."

"No, it isn't Dan. It's my brother, Riley."

"Wait, what?"

"Riley needs the help of the Iron Ladies." Loren was worried about him and Adeline, but it stemmed from the hopelessness of two lovers not being together.

"Is he hurt? Is Riley married and forgot to mention it?" Melanie's voice had turned very cold.

"No, nothing like that. He needs the help of the Iron Ladies—or rather, one Iron Lady in particular. My brother is brokenhearted, and I can't stand to see him like that. He's in love with Adeline, but for some reason, he believes that Adeline was only using him. He's trying to go on because that is what Adeline claims to want, but he's dying to hear from her, be with her. I can see it. He gets mad whenever I bring her up. Tell me please, do you know anything about the way Adeline feels? I thought she was falling in love with him too."

"Oh, she's in love, all right, she's just scared shitless. She's afraid that all men break hearts."

"Not Riley, he's one of the good ones."

"I agree." Melanie was quiet for a second before adding, "Okay, Loren, here's what we are going to do. "

*A*s normal Riley went to his sister's for dinner, and like normal, the house was nothing like her old one. Sure, she kept it clean and it was well-decorated, but it wasn't stuffy. Loren allowed Noelle to leave her toys anywhere she wanted, and there was a pile of mail on the counter and dishes in the sink. In other words, the house looked like a home and not a showplace.

"I have a favor to ask you."

Riley put his fork down, not liking the sound of that. He was used to his sister's different tones. "Uh-oh, what?"

"Well, I have a friend from college who wants to visit, she is single. I was wondering if while she is in town you could take her out for me. You know, show her a good time, since you aren't dating anyone."

"A blind date? No. Loren, don't. I'm busy."

"Don't be silly, you don't even know what day it is."

"It doesn't matter, I'll still be busy. I don't want to be set up on dates. I don't want to go out. I don't want to see anyone. Don't you get it? I actually cared about Adeline. I'm not ready."

"Then why don't you call her instead of moping around?"

"I'm not moping."

Loren raised one brow and stared Riley down.

"I hate that you've learned how to do that, you never used to challenge me. Fine. Whatever. Call it moping if you want but the fact still remains that I don't want to go out with any one. Besides I have something that I want to talk with you about."

"Sure, are you okay?"

"You are Noelle are doing great now and I can't tell you enough how proud I am of you. But the truth is, you don't need me. I always felt like you did when you were with Greg maybe it was because I didn't trust Greg. But whatever the reason, you're good now, Noelle is like a different kid already."

"What's your point? Because I'll always need you."

"You know that I bought some land in Montana several years ago?"

Loren nodded.

"Well, I think its time that I do something with it. I'm going to go up there for a while. I bought the land because it was in an upcoming snow ski area. I'm going to see what I can do with it, who knows."

Loren held up her hands in a surrender gesture, then stood to clear away Noelle's toys, including the teddy bear that held the hidden nanny-cam. Loren turned it off. There was no way in hell she could let Riley leave. He needed to be here, he needed to be with Adeline.

"COME ON, Noelle, we are going to go see if we can find Uncle Riley." Riley heard Loren talking as she pulled open the door to Keke's, but he didn't turn until he heard his niece.

"Uncle Wiley." Noelle ran to where he was seated and hopped onto his lap.

"What are you doing here, squirt?" Riley set Noelle to the side of him and looked up to his sister. "Have a meeting?"

"Yeah, need to drop some stuff off to the girls, and then Noelle and I are going to get mommy-daughter mani/pedis. So we decided to come in for some juice and a pastry. How about you? This isn't your side of town."

"I like the food here. So I come whenever I can." Just then a waitress set Riley's order of black coffee, coffee with cream and sugar, a bagel, a croissant, and a cup of fruit onto the table.

Loren took in the spread and rose an eyebrow. "Are you meeting someone? Are we *harshing your vibe*?"

"Don't. Don't go there, and don't ever say that again. I'm not meeting anyone. I order it just in case . . ."

"Just in case . . ." Riley really just wanted Loren to put the pieces together herself, so he stayed silent, waiting for the understanding to light her eyes. "Ohhh, is this what Adeline likes? You mean that you order her breakfast just in case she comes here?"

"Pitiful, I know."

"No, it's not. It's romantic. You need to call her. Stop torturing yourself."

"Loren, you know me. I have no problem sharing my feelings. But at the same time, I'm not a glutton for punishment. I took it slow so she could ease into the thought of a relationship, but she still ended it. I'm not going to throw myself out there again. She doesn't have to tell me more than once. Besides, actions speak way louder than words. She hasn't contacted me . . . that right there speaks loud and clear."

"What if she's saying the same thing? You have contacted her, actions speak louder than words?"

"She has no right, she ended it."

"Why are men so ignorant? I expected more from you, after all you're my brother. You've witnessed my life and what it's like for a woman to be scared and not loved. If there was a possibility of you and Adeline working out in the end wouldn't it be worth it to swallow your pride and try? Call me stupid but I just don't think that we have a limitless supply of soulmates. I think that we need to cherish the one that crosses our path."

Chapter Twenty-Seven

ADELINE

*A*deline woke up at a quarter after seven and was met with complete silence. There was no way the house should be quiet at this time of day, this was when they were all in full-throttle daily preparation mode. Hell, there should be a shower going and blow dryers humming and plates clattering into the sink. But the place was silent.

Melanie's door was open, and the bed was made, but there was no Melanie. She found the same in Sunday and Olivia's rooms as well. On her way to the kitchen, Adeline poked her head into the garage, only to find her car was the only one in the driveway.

She made coffee, growing more and more annoyed that no one had bothered to get her up, and by the time she was sliding into her Charger, she was well into angry.

That anger turned irrational when she walked into the office and found Melanie, Sunday, and Olivia in a meeting with Loren and little Noelle. A meeting she wasn't told about.

"Well, good morning, everyone. So glad that you were all able to make it in for the appointment. I'm sorry, Loren, but I didn't get the memo that you were going to be here."

Adeline shot daggers at her friends, disappointed in them and their utter lack of respect for her. They knew she had become friends with Loren, and they were meeting with her on the side, what was up with that shit?

"Loren is here to finalize a case," Melanie said.

"We closed the file for Loren's case a few weeks ago," Adeline reminded them, wondering why the hell Melanie had just lied to her.

"Not her case but another case that involved her. This one we went all-out for."

"Wait. You three took on a case without me? I didn't vote."

"The three of us voted, and it was a *yes,* so it didn't really matter whether you voted or not. Let's be frank, though, you haven't been in any condition to contribute to a case. You're barely taking care of yourself right now."

Melanie's words were like a slap to Adeline's face. "My opinion *didn't matter*? I'm sorry, did I miss something here?" Adeline thought back over the last few weeks, she hadn't been that bad, she was taking care of herself. Wasn't she? "Can you at least tell me about the case? Unless, of course, you three decided to take a vote and fire me."

"Don't be so dramatic. Yes, you are still one-fourth partner," Melanie assured her.

"Then I should have been included, or at least had the option," Adeline countered.

Olivia shrugged. "We thought it was more important that you used the time to clear your head. You have a lot on your mind right now, and we were worried that you wouldn't be able to give it your full attention."

Olivia's words only seemed to piss Adeline off even more. What did they think? Did they think she was worthless? Had they written her off as a team member? "I'm a grown woman, if I need space, I will tell you that I need space. I don't need you making that choice for me, or deciding that I'm incapable of *doing my job*. Have I ever not given a case my full focus? No, I always do. Have I ever not been a team player? No. But you three can't say the same. Our team is all four of us, so excluding one person fucks up the team."

Melanie sighed and then rolled her hand in the air as a signal to Sunday. Sunday slid a manila envelope across the table. Loren had stayed quiet. Adeline picked it up but didn't seem to be in a hurry as she glared at the women she considered her family.

Slowly, she lifted the flap, reached in, and pulled out several photos . . . of Riley.

"What the hell?"

Sunday clicked on her fucking computer, which Adeline wanted to hurl out the fucking window, while Melanie turned on the television screen and turned the volume up. When Riley's voice surrounded Adeline, it was like a pair of arms holding her. His deep tenor was familiar, but as she listened, she realized that something was off, something was wrong with Riley. At that thought, Adeline's head began to swim.

"Stop, Loren, I don't want to go out with anyone else. Okay. You don't get it? I was actually falling for Adeline." He scoffed. "Who am I kidding? I had fallen."

The pain in his voice took her breath away and wrapped around her ribs like a vice. The recording stopped, and the next one began.

"Hello? Riley? Are you okay?" Loren's groggy voice sounded through the recording.

"Yeah, I'm sorry, did I wake you?"

"Just a little, Ri, it's three in the morning. Is something wrong?"

"Sorry, I didn't realize what time it was. Go back to sleep."

"Riley, have you been drinking?"

"Yeah. I couldn't sleep." Adeline could hear the slight slur in Riley's words.

"Call her. Not tonight, but tomorrow. Call her tomorrow after eight in the morning."

The recording ended, and Sunday shut the program down.

Adeline didn't know when the recording was made, but Riley hadn't called her.

An image popped up on the screen of Riley sitting at a booth, *their* booth, at Keke's. Not once but several times. She could tell that this was different visits because every time Riley was there he was wearing a different shirt. And each time, the expression on his face looked a little more crestfallen. He seemed to be on the outskirts, not really taking in his surroundings...just there.

A tear rolled down Adeline's cheek. Adeline wasn't a crier. She hated women who cried, it was weak and she wasn't weak. But damn it, she was being betrayed by her own stupid tears as another one rolled down her cheek.

Then another video started to play, this one of Loren and Riley sitting on a couch. "She smelled like vanilla. I never eat vanilla, and now I find myself buying fucking vanilla ice cream every single day. The girl at Baskin Robbins probably thinks I'm hypoglycemic and constantly needing a sugar fix."

This was more than Adeline could bear. Throwing her hands over her face, she let the tears fall as they may. "I don't know what to do."

"Good thing you have us then, huh?" Melanie asked as she stood to turn the television off. "We're going to help but I have to tell you that Riley is leaving next week."

"Leaving? For how long?"

"A year or more. He's moving to Montana," Loren added.

"He can't. I need him. Where is he?"

"Just so happens, he's at Keke's for breakfast and I happen

to know that he orders enough for two people. He's been there since..."

"SEVEN." Adeline said before Melanie could finish.

"*Keke, do you love me?*" Olivia started singing, which was met by a group of moans and one pad of paper being tossed at her head. "What? Keke's has been around forever, and it just seems fitting that this song is all the rage right now and that it is Adeline and Riley's spot. You know that if everything works out, you'll have to name a kid Drake, or Olivia. I can handle Olivia." Adeline picked up her pen and flung it at Olivia as well.

For the first time in weeks, Adeline felt good. She had a plan, or rather that her plan was no fucking plan at all. She grabbed her purse and headed back to the elevator and then in under three minutes she was in her car and on her way to get her man.

Chapter Twenty-Eight

ADELINE

*A*deline had some old-school Poison playing at full volume, and as they were singing, "Something to Believe In," she pulled into the parking lot, cut the wheel, threw the gear shift into reverse, and slid into an open spot. God, she loved showing off. It was a sure sign that her day was

going to be good, it had to be because it had sucked lately without Riley.

Adjusting the rearview mirror so she could check herself once more, she added one more pass with her Devil Red signature lipstick, grabbed her purse, and hopped out. A few deep breaths, and she headed for the door.

Adeline didn't stop to take in the cars around her, but if she had, she would have seen four familiar vehicles pulling into different spots. Each one laughing at the other one when they rolled in because all there for the same reason...to see Adeline and Riley make up.

Pulling the door open to the restaurant, Adeline pushed her sunglasses onto her head and her eyes darted to the back corner booth. There sat the most gorgeous man she'd ever seen. She knew he was going to smell of spices and fresh-cut grass, and that his hands would have a slight callus to them, because he wasn't the type of man who got manicures, and he was the kind of man that worked with his hands. He was just Riley.

He must have sensed her because he looked up as she reached halfway. He stood but didn't move toward her.

Adeline told herself to keep walking, knowing that if she stopped, she would lose her nerve. The thought had a smile tugging on her lips. Adeline Morgan didn't lose her nerve.

She took the last fifteen or so steps toward Riley, and each one had a bit more of her reserve slipping away until she was hurling herself into his arms, and she let out the breath she didn't realize that she'd been holding when he caught her.

"You're here, you're finally here. I kept telling myself that you'd eventually show up."

"I'm here." Adeline giggled, holy hell she giggled like a fucking preteen schoolgirl.

"I'm going to kiss you."

But he didn't get to because she beat him to it, and whether Keke's was used to this crazy display of affection this early in the morning, no one knew, but they definitely were not used to the commotion going on outside their windows. Adeline pulled back from Riley and turned to see Olivia, Sunday, Melanie, Loren, and Noelle all shouting and clapping.

"They are nuts."

"They are," he said before dropping another kiss to her lips. "You hungry? I've already ordered."

Adeline bit her lip, feeling a little shy for the first time in her life, but she nodded and let him tug her down into the booth. "Yeah, I'm starved, but let's take it to go."

So they waited for their order to be packaged, seemingly unable to keep their hands from stealing little touches or their lips from seeking the other's out. When they finally walked outside, Adeline had to force herself not to drag him to her car and take what she wanted. First, sex in public at any time of day was ill-advised, and second, her car wasn't in the parking lot.

Her head whipped around, and her eyes were wide as she pulled herself from Riley's side.

"Riley, do you see my car?" Frantic. It was the only way to describe her voice. Her car was her baby, and she had parked it right in the spot where they currently stood.

She didn't wait for him to answer—she already knew her Charger wasn't where it was supposed to be—and pulled out her phone.

Then she froze.

MELANIE: Chill. I have your Charger. Olivia is following me home then she'll bring me back to get my car. Now you don't have a ride. You have no choice but to go with him. Have fun.

ADELINE LET out a chuckle and showed the message to Riley. "Well, your chariot awaits. My truck is over here."

Less than twenty minutes later they were walking into his house, and five minutes after that they were in his bedroom, clothes strewn across the floor.

Adeline splayed her hands out against his muscular chest and then dragged her nails down as she fell to her knees before him. Wrapping one hand around his hard shaft, she used her other to cup and play with his balls. The moan that escaped his lips was music to Adeline's ears. She rubbed her tongue around the base of the head and then up, sliding it across the tip and then back down the other side. Each stroke of her tongue brought a new sound from Riley, and Adeline found a power within her that she never knew she'd possessed until that moment.

When his hands slid to the back of her head and his fingers sank into her hair, a shiver rolled down her spine.

There was something powerful in being powerless as well.

She let him guide her, loved the feel of him sliding past her lips and hitting the back of her throat. Loved the deep rumble and half-formed praise that fell from his lips as she took him deeper, humming her own approval.

"Oh god, Adeline . . ." He thrust harder, fisted his hands in her hair a little tighter, and her hands found his hips, nails digging in and urging him on. "Fuck!"

His whole body tensed with his release, the splash of satisfaction coating her throat.

Adeline looked up and locked her eyes with Riley's honey-brown ones. She swallowed then brought one index finger up and wiped the corner of her mouth.

"I think that I just died and went to heaven." Riley pulled her up to stand next to him.

Adeline didn't answer him—hell, she wasn't sure that she even comprehended what he had said because she was too busy concentrating on his lips. She followed every movement, when he cracked a smile so did she. When he licked his lips, she mimicked the reaction. When he leaned in, she stepped back so she could watch as he lowered his head to her breasts and began to suck. He played with one hard nipple, the sweep of his tongue across the pebbly surface sent shivers racing down Adeline's spine.

"Riley." She moaned and trembled when he groaned, adding a slight vibration to her already sensitive breasts. Her breath was a mixture of blissful sighs and pleas for relief.

Adeline smiled as Riley made his intentions known, not verbally, but by using his mouth to coax her back toward the bed. A tug to the left on her sensitive nerves had Adeline following his movement. Allowing herself to be directed, she moved to the center of the bed slowly as Riley continued his assault, which was a mixture of soft bites, tugs, and kisses.

The cool air tickled her already heightened senses as Riley broke his contact with her nipple and moved his hands to the V of her thighs, driving one finger inside of her.

"Oh god, Riley."

When he raised his head Adeline focused on his eyes. She had never seen his eyes so dark or hooded with desire and she knew somehow, hers mirrored that desire. Adeline refused to break the hold he had on her even as he drove another finger inside of her several times, before bringing his fingers up to his own lips and sucking.

Adeline had never once contemplated eating pussy but right then, watching Riley do that, it had to be the hottest fucking move in the entire world. She was on fire. She was ready to explode any moment.

There was no holding back.

"That's it, baby, come for me." Riley's voice was heavy with desire.

Adeline writhed, almost thrashing as her orgasm tore through her. The muscles in her legs tightened and her back arched as the waves of aftershock washed through her, and she was left marveling at this man in front of her.

ADELINE FOUND it hard to remember what it was like to be part of a family. Sure, she had a family, she knew they used to do family things, but all those memories had been overshadowed by the tragedy of Sasha and then the drugs and rehab. Once she had rebelled, her parents distanced themselves from her. Hell, while she was in rehab, they bought her the house she lived in just so she wouldn't move back into their house once she was released. That should have hurt her, but truthfully, she was grateful. That single gesture had changed her life. It led her to her three best friends, which ultimately led her to Riley.

She and Riley had just spent the day with Noelle at the Magic Kingdom. Since Riley wasn't going to Montana, he was using a few days off to spend them with Adeline.

Adeline was laughing because Noelle had convinced her uncle that she needed shoes that matched almost every single princess. He'd turned to Adeline for help, but she was firmly on Team Noelle on this one. "A girl's gotta have shoes," was all Adeline kept saying.

Adeline had never thought that she'd want kids, but seeing Riley with his niece and hanging out with Noelle these last few weeks had changed her mind. She could seriously see a kid in her future . . . *their* future.

"Whatcha thinking about?" Riley wove his fingers between hers as they sat on the couch at his house. Noelle was asleep on a blanket on the floor as they waited for Loren to pick her up.

"Nothing, just thinking about how happy I am."

"Are you really happy?" Riley looked nervous.

"Yeah. You make me happy. I'm happy with my life and where this"—she waved her hands between her and Riley —"is going."

"Then move in with me. I have plenty of room. I know that you like living with the girls and if it's that then we'll find a house closer to them."

"No." Adeline saw the look of hurt on Riley's face and backpedaled. "No! I didn't mean that . . . I'm not saying no to moving in, it's that I'm saying no to moving close to them. The girls and I have spoken so many times about selling that house. None of us truly like it or the area. It was just kind of where we landed out of convenience. If anything, I'd rather they move out here. We've actually looked at office space over near Medical City. We like it over there because it's close to the gun range and most of our training areas."

"So then that's a yes?"

"Yes, but only if you're sure. I don't know if you've truly thought this through. I come with a lot of baggage. I mean . . . I come with three grown-ass girls. They will be popping around and checking in on us."

"So will my sister."

"I have a lot of shoes."

"I have tons of closet space." Riley winked, not at all put off by any of Adeline's reasons.

"I have girly stuff."

"I have guy stuff, and as soon as Loren gets here, I will show you exactly what my guy stuff can do to your girly stuff."

Adeline let out a low laugh. This feeling, the one that she felt when she was with Riley, oh yeah, it was love, that's what that feeling was. Anyway, it was more intoxicating than any drink or any drug and Adeline knew one thing for sure: she wanted to be high on it forever.

EPILOGUE

$\mathcal{T}$hree years later . . .

ADELINE HELD her notepad in one hand and her pen in the other. She had an army of men helping her today. They were carrying boxes into the new Iron Ladies headquarters. It was nestled at the front of the five-thousand-acre parcel of land that the former mayor of Orlando thought he could trick Adeline's husband into selling to the city for dirt cheap. The compound, as Adeline liked to call it, was divided into four parts.

The residences, which were four different houses nestled into one section of the property.

The training grounds, which included an indoor gun range, a small racetrack, and a gym. The counseling center, which had a licensed counselor on call to meet with the women during the whole investigation and divorce process. The offices, which included the Iron Ladies' office as well as the law office, which was run by Barrett Huxley. He'd left the law firm he had been working at so that he could work with the girls full time. He liked to tease and say that he was *The Man in the Iron Mask*. But it was nice having him around for legal advice and to help with messy cases.

"Put that over there. Nope, I said over there." Adeline pointed to a stack of boxes in the corner, and Riley let out a groan.

"Fine, I'll do it myself." Adeline threw her notepad and pen down and walked over to grab the box, but Riley stopped her and threw his arms around her large pregnant belly.

"Uh-huh. No you don't, Mrs. Thomas, you are due any day so you are not lifting any boxes. I'll pick it back up and move it." He bent and kissed Adeline's belly. "He isn't ready to come out, so don't force him."

"I'm not having a boy, it's a girl."

"You're having a boy, there's no way God would be so cruel. I'm surrounded by women. You, your friends, my sister, Noelle. I need a boy. I need some male bonding." Riley threw his hands up as if he were in prayer. "Please."

Adeline laughed. She knew what they were having, but she wasn't telling him. They had agreed not to find out, but Adeline couldn't stand the not knowing. She'd decided that she liked the name Drake Thomas after all.

Sunday Prescott was a tech goddess, cyber espionage was her specialty. During her latest assignment, she uncovered more than she ever hoped for: Bo Camden. Find out if she will sleep with the enemy or get her sweet vengeance, ***Sunday, Sweet Vengeance***. Tap on the title to purchase or keep reading for a sneak peek.

. . .

KEEP READING to find links to all of my books.

YOU WILL ALSO LIKE...

Iron Orchids Series

Get the series that started them all—immerse yourself in the world of the Iron Orchids. #notagang. Get started with Ariel, Always Enough, for FREE.

Iron Horse Series

Want more hot cops and strong women? Get London's story in London, Is Falling.

A WORD FROM DANIELLE

Thank you for picking up my book. It doesn't matter whether you have read one book of ten written by me, they all have some commonalities to them:

Strong women with attitude.

Alpha heroes who love them anyway.

And a strong bond of friendship that we all need in our lives.

The Iron Orchids, books 1 through 6, were my original series of romance novels. Each book can be read as a stand-alone. What connects the stories are the fact the same people appear and eventually each gets their own Happily Ever After.

So if you've read one then you are probably dying to read about the rest of the brothers and their missing cousin.

Read on to find sneak peeks from some of the books along with my suggested reading order.

Thank you again - Dani

Suggested Reading Order Including Excerpts

ORIGINAL IRON ORCHIDS, BOOKS 1 THROUGH 6

TAP THE LINKS TO FIND THE TITLE IN YOUR FAVORITE STORE

Ariel, Always Enough - Book 1
Sophie, Almost Mine - Book 2
Katy, My Impact - Book 3
Leo, Kiss Often - Book 4
Stella, Until You - Book 5
Christine, The Stars - Book 6

IRON ORCHIDS—BADGES SERIES, BOOKS 7 THROUGH 11

You met some of them in the Iron Orchids. Now these women motorcycle officers will ride into your heart.

Badges Prequel - Book 7
Sadie, Doctor Accident - Book 8
Bridget, Federal Protection - Book 9
Piper, Unlikely Outlaw - Book 10
Kat, Knight Watch - Book 11 (April 7, 2020)

IRON LADIES, BOOKS 1 AND 2

A whisper network of women. Women who help the wives of controlling men. You don't want to cross these ladies.

Adeline, Getting Even - Book 1
Sunday, Sweet Vengeance - Book 2

IRON HORSE, BOOKS 1 THROUGH 3

The love stories of three sisters who struggle to run a cattle ranch and to prove the strongest cowboys can be a girl.

London, Is Falling - Book 1
Paris, In Love - Book 2
Holland, At War - Book 3

SUNDAY, SWEET VENGEANCE

Book 2, Iron Orchids—Ladies

Chapter 1 - Sunday

Seven years later . . .

"He could eat cookies in my bed anytime." The soft voice came from behind a quad monitor stack. "Oh, and by the way, I just changed my name to Cookie." Sunday Prescott wiped the corner of her mouth to make sure she wasn't drooling.

Her three best friends laughed as they sat at their desks. Since their office was an open-floor plan they were used to her monologues as she read over the latest Hollywood gossip. It was her daily guilty pleasure, and she loved flipping through the different sites to see what was being said and who was taking up the headlines of page six. "Why can't we get a case like this?" Sunday asked, not really expecting an answer as she moved on to the next headline. Her friends had learned not to get too invested in the news because, by the time they were ready to ask questions, Sunday was reading something else. "Don't you worry about that, Duchess, we'll come to you. If he's like his daddy, we'll nail his ass. Don't let him hurt you or those babies."

"Sunday," Adeline Morgan snapped.

"What?"

"Close that shit. I have no clue why you read that stuff."

"And I have no clue why you don't. You know that whole saying about walk a mile in someone else's shoes? Well, I'm reading a mile, and believe me, I'm happy right where I am."

"You do realize that most of those stories are fake, right? Those sites spread lies and shit about people and create drama and tension for the sole purpose of sewing doubt within their subjects' relationships, which usually causes something that had been solid to unravel." Melanie waved her finger to emphasize unraveling. "How many times can you read that your man is having an affair before you start believing it? Then when the couple splits, the gossip site is all, "See, we told you this was going to happen! You heard it here first."

"I could never be married to someone famous," Olivia said. "I'd be in prison for either shooting the lying journalist or my cheating man. I just don't have the temperament for it."

Sunday stood and looked around the monitors, a sardonic smile on her lips. "You think? And here I thought you were so mild-mannered." Sunday winked to let Olivia know that she was totally joking. The gesture was unnecessary because anyone who knew Sunday would know the girl didn't have a cruel bone in her body.

"Hey, while we have Sunday's head up from her wall of gossip sites, our client will be here in about thirty minutes." Melanie, the ever-professional one, slid each of the women a thin stack of papers. "Her name is Traci Camden, co-owner of Camden Financial."

"Shit, she and her husband are always in the paper like some picture perfect couple," Adeline whispered. "By all accounts, the Camdens are happily married billionaires."

Adeline stuck one finger in her mouth as if she was gagging. "Smoke and mirrors, guarantee it."

Sunday cleared her throat, interjecting, "The fuck you say?"

"Gee, Sunday, with a mouth like that you should be a preschool teacher," Adeline teased.

"I just wish y'all would make up your minds. First you say that the media makes everyone look bad and rips relationships apart, but now Adeline is saying they make a horrid couple look good. Y'all are seriously fucked up."

"Can we go back to that billion dollars? Someone explain to me how one accrues a billion dollars. I mean, seriously, that's a lot of whack. We're talking ten digits, right?" Olivia flipped her fingers up one at a time so she could count. "Yep, ten digits."

"It's his worth, not what he has in the bank," Adeline stated. "So, we're talking about the value of his properties, business value, investment portfolios, and liquid assets. A lot of time, these asshats have a net worth of a billion and a debt of almost a billion. Crazy mother fuckers, if you ask me. Who wants that kind of debt?"

Sunday closed the gossip rag sites and began a basic search for Kai and Traci Camden to see if she could find anything that would hint as to why Mrs. Camden would suddenly be in need of their services.

FIND ME

Website: www.daniellenorman.com

Official Iron Orchids Reading Group : www.daniellenorman.-com/group

Sign up for Danielle's Newsletter and stay in the know
Newsletter: www.daniellenorman.com/news

Go to your App Store and download the app called Danielle Norman or visit
app.daniellenorman.com to download from the internet.

MEET DANIELLE

It is amazing what can happen over a glass of vodka. Danielle Norman knows all too well since that's how she was convinced to try writing a romance novel. A few more sips and seventy-thousand words later she was falling in love.

Her books have sold in more than two-hundred countries and her first book in the Iron Orchids series, *Ariel: Always Enough* has been downloaded more than two million times. It was a bestseller on Amazon and hit #1 on Apple Books and Barnes & Noble.

Danielle embraces her motto, *Romance with Attitude*.

THANK YOU

- Editing by AW Editing
- Proofreading by Deaton Author Services
- Proofreading by Taryn Lawson
- Cover Design by F Squared LLP

Well hell's bells here we are again with another fucking book finished. As much as I'd like to say that I did it all myself I can't. Just like it takes a village to raise a snot-nose brat, it takes an army to produce a book.

Thank you Ashley- Who vs that...really? Is it such a big deal? LOL. Some day I'm going to get all of this right and you are going to miss the little shit.

To Beluga Vodka's distribution department...you suck. Your distillery produces the best vodka I've ever had and yet you can't get it distributed. Hello McFLY, people need to find it to buy it.

To the Iron Orchids, you bitches rock.

Printed in Great Britain
by Amazon

43398376R00139